She'd nev

consciou

It was as if

to being a very young teenager again, hormones racing all out of control.

He was barring her way. "Are we going to call a truce, Charlotte?"

"A truce?" She looked up at him uncertainly.

"Well, we can't go on like this, can we?"

"I don't know what you mean."

"I think you do. I'm sorry about what's happened."

She wondered which particular thing he was sorry about—notching her up on his bedpost or accusing her stepmother of fraud?

KATHRYN ROSS was born in Zambia, where her parents happened to live at that time. Educated in Ireland and England, she now lives in a village near Blackpool, Lancashire. Kathryn is a professional beauty consultant, but writing is her first love. As a child she wrote adventure stories, and at thirteen was editor of her school magazine. Happily, ten writing years later, *Designed with Love* was accepted by Harlequin Presents®. A romantic Sagittarian, she loves traveling to exotic locations.

Kathryn Ross

BLACKMAILED BY THE BOSS

TORONTO • NEW YORK • LONDON
AMSTERDAM • PARIS • SYDNEY • HAMBURG
STOCKHOLM • ATHENS • TOKYO • MILAN • MADRID
PRAGUE • WARSAW • BUDAPEST • AUCKLAND

ISBN 0-373-18846-3

BLACKMAILED BY THE BOSS

First North American Publication 2005.

This edition published by arrangement with Harlequin Books S.A.

www.eHarlequin.com

Printed in U.S.A.

CHAPTER ONE

THERE was no excuse, it was probably one of the most stupid things she had ever done in her life—apart from getting involved with David of course, that went without saying, but this… Her thoughts trailed off. This was incomprehensible it was so stupid.

She turned her head slightly on the pillow and looked across to the other side of the bed. They had left the bedside lamp on last night, so she could see him quite clearly—it hadn't been a dream, he was still there and fast asleep. Charlotte felt panic rising like a spring inside her, gushing like iced water through her veins. Jordan was her father's business partner, for heaven's sake; and more than that he was her boss. How could she have let this happen?

Her eyes drifted over his features; he looked different asleep, less formidably handsome…more vulnerable. It was an absurd thought; Jordan Lynch was anything but vulnerable; in fact he was one tough cookie, a dynamic businessman with a never-ending stream of glamorous girlfriends who just seemed to fall at his feet. Charlotte had watched them come and go and she had sworn she would never be one of his conquests. So what had happened? It wasn't even as if she could blame it on drink—two glasses of sparkling water was hardly mind-altering.

She cast her mind back to yesterday. She remembered her eyes had connected with his through the glass partition of the office. And she remembered thinking that he had the sexiest eyes on earth, before hurriedly looking away again. But that wasn't so unusual; she was a red-blooded woman after all, and very often she'd glance at Jordan and admire the sheer male perfection of him. But it didn't mean anything, it was a transitory thought that probably went through every woman's head at least once when they looked at him.

She had applied herself back to her work, reminding herself that he may be thirty-eight, single, wealthy and gorgeous, but his latest girlfriend was a twenty-three-year-old sultry Latin-American model. And anyway he wasn't her type—he was too arrogantly sure of himself; good-looking but knew it.

In fact Charlotte had quite enjoyed pretending she didn't notice him. Being coolly dismissive when everyone else was fawning around him appealed to her rebellious side. She hadn't particularly agreed with her father taking him on as a partner last year. They had been doing fine without him, then along he'd come with his newfangled ideas and his haughty manner. The first couple of months the air had been a bit frosty between them. But since then things had thawed slightly. To be honest, she'd had to get on with him because her father was rarely here these days and Jordan was running the show.

Then the phone on her desk had rung…

She'd ignored it, thinking her assistant, Frank, would pick it up in the main office. But it had continued to ring until in desperation she'd snatched it up. 'Charlotte McCann speaking; how may I help?'

'Hi, Charlie, it's Melanie. Just thought I'd touch base with you, see how you are. Bearing up, I hope?'

'Oh…hi, Melanie.' Charlotte's heart sank as she heard the sympathetic tones radiating from the other end of the line. Everyone was talking to her like that these days. She knew people meant well but she hated it. 'I take it you've heard?'

'Yes, Erica told me. I couldn't believe it; David always seemed such a solid, dependable type.'

Something twisted inside Charlotte. 'Yes, well, obviously appearances can be deceptive.'

'I'm really sorry, Charlie. You must be devastated.'

'Not really. Actually I'm feeling pretty positive about the situation; it's probably for the best.' Charlotte scribbled her pen rather violently through a memo Frank had left on her desk. 'Things had been cooling between us for some time now.'

'Even so, it's tough when a relationship ends,' Melanie purred. 'Listen, why don't you come for supper tomorrow? I'm having a lot of the girls over and it would be lovely to see you.'

And talk about the entire story in gory detail, Charlotte finished for her silently. She didn't want that—she'd rather forget it. 'It's a bit short notice, Mel... I'm pretty tied up—'

'Now, listen, it would do you good. Cindy Smith will be here and Janice Pike, and you haven't seen them for ages.' Melanie cut across her in a no-nonsense tone.

Janice Pike! Biggest gossip in London! Charlotte shuddered as she imagined what the evening would be like. They might as well bring along a bright light and a pair of thumbscrews to make it complete.

'It's not that...' She paused as Jordan came into the office and she mouthed to him that she wouldn't be a minute.

He perched on the edge of her desk, looking very suave in a dark suit with a pristine white shirt beneath. She probably should have taken that as a signal to hang up, but she ignored him, telling herself that she could take a few minutes to chat to a friend when she was always in the office half an hour earlier and half an hour later than anybody else.

'So what is it?' Mel persisted, never one to give in easily.

Charlotte took a deep breath and improvised wildly. 'The fact is, I'm seeing someone and it's early days…you know what it's like when you're in the "getting to know someone" stage.'

'Well, yes…' Melanie sounded stunned.

She noticed that even Jordan looked surprised—his dark eyebrows rose slightly.

'Gosh, that was quick, Charlie!' Mel drawled. 'I must say, you don't hang about.'

'Well, it is four and a half weeks since David and I split up.' As soon as she said the words she knew they were a mistake. When you were still counting the days, did it mean you weren't over someone? 'Anyway, I'm going to have to go, Mel.' She tried to wind up the conversation before she made things worse. 'Jordan has just walked into my office and I mustn't delay him.' That, at least, was the truth.

'Sorry about that,' she said as she put the phone down. 'Now, I've got those details ready about the latest designs, and I'm happy to say it's all coming on really well.' As she spoke she was running an eye over the drawings that lay before her on the desk.

'I didn't know you were dating someone new.' Jordan ignored her words and instead zoomed in on the very thing she wanted to gloss over.

She hesitated and for a moment contemplated lying to him as well, and then shrugged. What was the point in pretending?

'I'm not.' She didn't glance up; instead she shuffled the papers in front of her, trying to get back to the work. 'I want to talk to you about the budget for the new scheme—'

But Jordan wouldn't let the subject go. 'So why did you tell someone you were dating?' he persisted, stopping her in her tracks.

'Because…' she leaned back in her chair, running a flustered hand through her long blonde hair. 'Well, I suppose I didn't want Melanie to know that the most exciting thing I've done recently is watch a rerun of *Dallas* and order a take-away pizza.' The truth just popped out and she was surprised by his reaction because he seemed to relax somewhat, as if he found it terribly amusing.

'Oh, I see.'

'Not that I haven't had offers, of course,' she continued swiftly, feeling cross with herself for telling *him* that. 'But I've just been too bogged down with all of this.' She flicked the work in front of her derisively.

'Yeah, I know you've been working very hard,' he replied seriously.

Something about the way he looked at her set off a prickle of awareness inside that was deeply disturbing.

'Anyway, I know I'm nearly over budget on the curtaining for these apartments.' She returned the conversation very firmly to work. It wasn't the first time he'd had that effect on her and she supposed it wouldn't be the last. But it didn't mean anything; it was because he was a predatory male, and she read the danger signals loud and clear.

'But I want to use the more expensive sheer muslin for the front windows. I mean, what's the point of building somewhere with fabulous views and then spoiling it with the window dressing? It's like buying a fantastically expensive dress and teaming it with horrid shoes. Spoils the whole image.' She looked up and fixed him with wide, fervent green eyes. 'So can I up the budget?'

'Again?' His voice was dry. 'What are you doing, gold-plating the whole apartment block?'

'The windows will sell the place,' Charlotte said firmly. 'Women will walk into those apartments and fall in love with them at first sight.'

'That's what it takes, is it—good window dressing?'

Jordan grinned. 'OK,' he shrugged, 'you're the interior designer. I'll go with your recommendation and I'll up the budget.'

'Great—'

'On one condition.' He cut across her.

'What?'

'Have dinner with me tonight.'

The invitation took her aback. She looked up into his hazel eyes and all sorts of warning bells rang. 'I can't, Jordan. I'm sorry, but I've far too much on.'

'One evening won't make much difference on the work schedule. And anyway, there are a few things I think we should talk about.'

She had been left unsure as to whether he was asking her out to discuss business or asking her out on a date.

Charlotte freeze-framed the memory now as she lay in bed. She was still unsure about that.

She stared at the ceiling and analysed that invitation. They'd eaten together a few times over the last year, usually business lunches, sometimes with her father, sometimes alone. They'd never ended up naked in bed together the next morning!

Jordan moved in the bed, rolling over onto his side so that he was facing her. For a moment she thought he was waking up and her nerves jangled alarmingly, her heart pumping as if she'd been running on the treadmill at the gym. He settled down and continued to sleep. She noticed how dark his hair was against the white of the pillow, and how the sheets had slipped from his shoulders, revealing a tanned torso that was enticingly muscled. Remembering how tenderly those strong arms had held her last night, she felt her stomach dip in another pang of alarm.

This was terrible. She didn't want to think about what had actually transpired. She was going to have to get out of here, and fast, before he woke up. Because she couldn't face him. The whole thing was mortifyingly embarrassing.

Slipping a foot out of the bed, she sidled across from beneath the covers, trying to ease herself out so as not to create a sound or a draught. She ended up on her hands and knees on his floor and there she crouched for a few moments, trying to get her breath back, casting her eyes frantically around for her clothes.

Even as she was kneeling there she registered the ridiculousness of the situation. She was a thirty-two-year-old businesswoman, for heaven's sake—in fact, thirty-three in a few months' time—and here she was, almost hiding under a man's bed! She needed to be adult about this, she reasoned with herself. People had sex these days and they didn't agonise about it, they just enjoyed it.

But the logical words didn't cut much ice with her. Trouble was, she had never got with the modern programme—had never done the casual-sex bit. She needed to be in love with a man before she slept with him. All right, it was old-fashioned, but that was just how she was. So what had happened to change that last night?

She heard the bed creak as Jordan moved again. Her head shot up as she saw his hand dangling over the side, almost touching the top of her blonde curls. Any moment now he was going to lean over and ask her what she was doing crouching on his floor.

She waited for it, prepared to lie that she was looking for her contact lenses. But she didn't wear contact lenses, and he probably knew that.

Taking a deep breath, she forced herself to stand up. She needn't have worried—he was still asleep, this time sprawled over onto her side of the bed. Not that it was her bed, or her apartment. Darting a look around the room for her clothes, she could only see his shirt on a chair, so she picked it up and held it in front of her. At the same time

Jordan's hand seemed to be searching in the small space beside him, then he opened his eyes.

'Hi.' He smiled at her sleepily, then sat up slightly, his eyes moving over the long length of her legs to the shirt she held in front of her.

She, on the other hand, found her eyes drawn to his chest, which was broad and hairy and brought memories from last night trickling through her consciousness like red-hot lava.

'Are you OK?' he asked huskily.

She transferred her gaze quickly to his face to find his eyes resting on her with a kind of tender concern.

'Of course I'm OK.'

He raked a hand through the thick darkness of his hair. 'It's just…well, I thought you were on the floor for a moment.'

'I always start the day with a good crawl around on the bedroom floor.' She hadn't planned the sarcasm—it just slipped out. 'It helps to tone the body.'

He smiled. 'Your body doesn't need much toning,' he murmured, looking admiringly at the shapely long legs and the curves that were now hidden behind his shirt.

'I was looking for my clothes, actually.' Her voice seemed to have risen two octaves.

'I think you'll find them in the lounge, but what's the hurry?' He glanced at the illuminated numbers on his bedside clock. 'It's only early.'

How could he be so relaxed? As if this was nothing? Wasn't he even the slightest bit embarrassed? OK, maybe he was used to waking up with different women in the morning, but they had to work together, for heaven's sake!

Before she could reply the telephone on the other side of the bed rang. As he rolled over to answer it Charlotte glanced through the open bedroom door and caught sight of her clothes lying in a heap on the lounge floor. Thank heavens for phones, she thought as she hurriedly launched herself out through the door before he could turn around. Firmly she closed it behind her.

Never had she dressed as quickly in her whole life. Pants, stockings, skirt were all put on with record-breaking speed. Then, just as things were going so well, she couldn't find her bra. She looked along the cream leather settee and lifted a few cushions, but still couldn't find it. Hearing the phone go down in the other room, she gave up and instead threw her blouse on, buttoning it up with scant regard for anything other than the need to escape. Her bag was on the coffee-table, and the only thing hanging up was her coat out on a stand in the hallway. She practically flew to it, then out through the front door. Not waiting for the lifts, she ran down the stairs of the luxury apartment block as if being pursued by the devil himself.

It was only when she was outside in the cool darkness of the early-morning air that she realised she had no car. She had taken a taxi to meet Jordan at the restaurant last night and then they had walked back to his place.

She put her head down as it started to rain and turned towards the nearest underground station.

It was rush hour. Charlotte stood well to the right on an escalator that trundled slowly down into the bowels of the earth; a never-ending stream of people hurried past her, their shoulders brushing against hers, but she was barely aware of them. There was a constant thundering sound as trains sped through the passages below and a warm vortex of air spiralled upwards, blow-drying the rain from her blonde hair. Charlotte felt numb, as if she wasn't really there.

How could she have done that? she kept asking herself. How could she?

A busker stood in one of the tunnels, his voice echoing eerily as he sang about how much love hurt. The sound was accompanied by the silvery clinking of the coins that people threw on the way past. Maybe, like her, they agreed with his sentiment. Charlotte dug deep in her pockets and added her coins to his collection.

She had found out from David just how much love could hurt.

Maybe that was the reason some people…like Jordan…abandoned the idea of love completely and chose to just concentrate on the physical side of things. She had never really agreed with that way of thinking before, but now…now she wasn't sure how she felt about anything. Because buried away in the deepest recess of her mind was the knowledge that last night had been extremely pleasurable.

There was a train waiting on her platform and she raced towards it, just squeezing in before the automatic doors closed. She stood, hemmed in by the sheer volume of people, and grabbed at a handrail to steady herself as the train left the station. Then she closed her eyes and thought again back to last night.

She had insisted on meeting him at the restaurant. Somehow arriving under her own steam had made her feel more in control of the situation. It meant she would be able to leave when she wanted instead of having to wait for him. Charlotte liked to be independent.

They had started off talking about work. Jordan had made her laugh; he had a very dry, very witty sense of humour. She remembered a few women had cast envious eyes over towards their table and she had felt almost proud to be the one who was getting his undivided attention.

She realised now, that should have been her first warning signal.

'So where is your girlfriend tonight?' she had asked him when there was a pause in the conversation.

'Benita and I split up a couple of weeks ago.'

'Oh! I'm sorry.'

He shrugged. 'These things happen—as you know. Have you seen anything of David recently?'

She shook her head. 'I think he's still in the States on business.'

'Do you still have feelings for him?'

The intensely personal question took her aback and she hesitated, not knowing what to say.

'According to your father, he was never right for you.' Jordan filled the gap drily.

'Has my father been discussing my private life with you?' She was instantly annoyed.

'Only in passing.' He shrugged easily. 'You went out with David for a long time, didn't you.'

'Two years. How long were you with Benita?' Swiftly she changed the subject back in his direction.

Jordan frowned. 'I don't know; I'm not one for counting much any more.'

'Any more?'

'When I was married to Nadine I used to count anniversaries, important dates—you know, the usual kind of thing.'

His statement intrigued her. She had heard he had been divorced, but that was all, because Jordan was extremely aloof when it came to talking about his past. Charlotte had assumed, because he seemed such a womaniser, that he had ended the marriage. 'It sounds as if you loved her very much.'

'I did.' His voice was heavy. 'But it didn't do me a lot of good. Sometimes loving someone isn't enough.'

'Well, she was obviously just the wrong person for you.'

He smiled at that. 'You're not going to go all Pollyanna-like on me, are you?'

'No.' She felt herself blushing and he smiled.

'I've enjoyed tonight, Charlie; thank you.'

'I've enjoyed it too.' She was aware that she didn't really want the evening to end.

Jordan took out his wallet to pay the bill and she fumbled for her handbag.

'We'll go Dutch,' she said firmly.

'Dutch?' He stared at her as if she was speaking that language.

'Yes. I like to pay my own way, thank you.'

His lips twisted in a wry curve. 'Well you can pay next time,' he said dismissively, putting his credit card on the silver salver. 'How's that?'

Before she could make a reply to that he had switched the subject. 'Have you heard anything from your father recently?'

'Not since Ruth rang to tell me they wouldn't be coming home from France at the appointed time. Dad must really love it out there because it's not like him to want to take extra time off work. You know what he's like, a complete workaholic.'

'And she didn't say anything else?'

'No. It was a very brief conversation, but then it always is with my stepmother. She's usually in a hurry.' Charlotte frowned. 'Why?'

'I just wondered.' The waiter brought the counterfoil for him to sign. 'You get on all right with Ruth, don't you?' he asked casually as he handed the piece of paper and the pen back.

'Yes. She seems to make Dad happy.' She paused and frowned. 'Everything is all right with Dad, isn't it? You have spoken to him since he's been away?'

'Of course.' Jordan rose smoothly to his feet. 'He is my business partner; he couldn't be away for seven weeks without being in contact.'

He had put his hand at her back as they had walked out

of the restaurant. It had just been a light touch but Charlotte had been extremely conscious of it.

The train jerked to a halt and her eyes flew open. It was her station; she struggled to step out, battling amongst the hordes getting in.

The April rain was cold against her skin as she emerged again onto the streets above. But her mind was still tuned into the night before. They had walked back towards his apartment and he had invited her in for coffee. 'You may as well wait for a taxi in the comfort of my place,' he had said easily.

So she had followed him up to the stylish penthouse apartment. She had never been to his home before, and it had felt different being somewhere with him that wasn't work-related at all. It had made her suddenly self-conscious. And when he had reached to take her coat, she had felt more acutely aware of him than she had ever done.

As he disappeared through to the kitchen to make the coffee she had wandered around the lounge, admiring the décor. 'Who did the interior design to this apartment?' She called out the question to him through the open door.

'I don't know. I wasn't particularly interested in interior designers until I met you.'

She smiled at the compliment. Then noticed a photograph of a little girl, about three years of age, with dark shiny hair and a mischievous grin.

'Who is this?' she asked as Jordan came back through to the lounge.

'That's my daughter, Natasha.'

'I didn't know you had a child! She looks adorable.'

'Yes.' He put the tray of coffee down on the table and then went over towards her. 'She was adorable.' He reached out a hand and took the photograph from her.

'Was?' Charlotte had a cold feeling inside as she heard

the ominous tone in his voice and saw for a moment raw emotion in the darkness of his eyes.

'She died almost two years ago.'

'I'm so sorry, Jordan.'

She watched as he carefully put the photograph back where it had been. And in that instant she wanted to reach out to him, soothe the shadows from his face. Jordan was always so controlled, so confident; she had never seen that rawness of expression on his face before. Instinctively she reached up and touched him, trailing her fingers in a soft caress along the side of his cheek.

He caught her hand in his and then, as their eyes met, the unguarded emotion changed into something else, and he turned the hand to kiss the inside of her wrist. The gesture was totally unexpected and there was something extremely provocative and yet sensitive about it…something that made her insides turn over.

'You look beautiful tonight,' he murmured, and his eyes moved over her body in the softly flattering blue suit. 'But then, you always look beautiful.'

She raised questioning eyes to his. There had always been some kind of turbulent chemistry between them; maybe subconsciously that was why she had always kept a distance from him. Because she knew he spelt danger. But now that feeling of danger was teamed with something else, something much more powerful. She felt it spiralling inside her like a spinning top, whipping around and around in her insides. And she wondered what it would be like to kiss him.

He had reached out and touched her face the way she had his and the touch had been like a spark to a can of petrol because the next thing she remembered she had stood on tiptoe to kiss him.

She had made the first move.

Remembering that made her heart stand still.

After the initial moment of surprise he had kissed her back. And what a kiss that had been! Just thinking about it now made her insides clench with desire again. Jordan Lynch knew exactly the right way to kiss a woman. His lips had travelled over hers with a slow, seductive warmth that had been so deliriously wonderful it had made her toes curl.

As passion exploded quickly out of control, there had been a moment when Jordan had pulled back. 'Are you sure about this?' he had asked seriously.

She had smiled and reached to kiss him again.

Remembering that now made Charlotte's skin burn.

Hurriedly she let herself into her flat and leaned back against the door. She was faced with her familiar, modern, perfectly designed home, but it felt different to her now. It was as if the person who had left here last night was not the same person who had returned. It was as if she didn't know herself any more.

The phone rang on the hall table and her nerves jumped. Would that be Jordan? She didn't answer it and after a few moments the answering machine clicked in.

'Hi, sweetheart, it's David. I hoped I'd catch you before you left for work. Look, I just wanted to tell you again how sorry I am. It was one night, honey, and it didn't mean anything, not compared with my love for you. It was a mistake, a terrible mistake, a moment of insanity. Anyway...' His voice trailed off, became more hopeless than eager. 'I'm flying back to England tomorrow. I'll call you then.'

The earnest, pleading voice touched the far recesses of her mind. Yesterday she wouldn't have understood a moment of insanity, but yesterday she had been a sensible person and now...now she didn't know what the hell she was doing any more.

CHAPTER TWO

HIS timing was wrong. Jordan knew that, he'd known it last night but he hadn't been able to stop himself. He disliked himself intensely for the weakness. Yet perversely he didn't regret it. Charlotte had been everything he'd dreamed she'd be; passionate, warm…it had been intensely pleasurable. How could he regret that?

He reached for his briefcase and climbed out of his car. When should he tell her? he wondered. Today wouldn't be right, not now. He was grimly aware that he was putting off the inevitable again. Charlotte was going to find out, and sooner rather than later, whether he told her or not. It was better that she heard it directly from him and not through a third party. But not today.

The sky was a heavily leaden grey. It was reflected in the choppy waters of the River Thames and the modern glass building that was the central administrative centre for McCann Developments.

Charlotte's grandfather, George McCann, had started the business years before. He was a builder who had worked his way up from small beginnings to create a successful development firm of good repute. Charlotte's father, Simon, had taken over the running of the place twenty-five years ago and things had ticked along fairly well until they had hit the recession five years ago, leading to dwindling profits and eventually the necessity of taking on Jordan as a partner.

Being the newcomer on the block hadn't been as easy as Jordan had anticipated. But he was a talented architect and an experienced businessman with a nose for a good deal. He'd been here for just over a year and already the profits were up. Along the way he'd had to make a few changes to streamline the running of the place, and he knew that even more changes were necessary if the business was to thrive.

His thoughts went to Simon McCann. He admired him and the business was sound. That was the reason he had invested in it in the first place, but just recently he had noticed a change in Simon. He had become reluctant to look at new designs that were essential for them to keep ahead of the opposition. It was almost as if he had lost his enthusiasm. And it was becoming more apparent that if Jordan was to make any real inroads into the success of the business he would need to have the casting vote.

It was coming to crunch time, when he might be forced to get Simon to sell his share of the business to give him overall control, and he didn't think Charlotte would be too happy about that.

Added to all of that there was the matter of the missing money.

'Morning, Jordan.' His secretary paused to wait for him by the lifts in the front lobby.

'Morning, Laura.' He smiled back at the attractive brunette, but in truth his mind was skipping ahead to his meeting with Charlotte. Wondering how he should play things after last night.

His eyes were drawn to the brass plaque in the lift, with the name McCann Developments. He wondered how Charlotte would feel if the business ceased to be a family affair. Somehow, he thought she wouldn't be too pleased.

Charlotte had started work here six years ago and was in charge of the interior-design side of the business. When Jordan first met her he had found her a bit prickly—had thought that she was probably a spoilt little rich girl who had got a job here purely through nepotism.

In reality he couldn't have been further from the truth. He had discovered she was an exceptionally talented designer who worked extremely hard and had once owned her own successful interior-design business. Her father had persuaded her to join the family company by promising her much bigger and more lucrative projects. As well as designing the interior of their show houses she ran an after-sales service for customers who wanted their homes bringing up to the same high standards. This was proving so successful that they'd had to expand the company's design section.

No, somehow he couldn't see Charlotte being pleased if her father was to leave the business.

As soon as he stepped out onto the top floor of the office he saw that she was already seated at her desk. He'd half wondered if she would be late this morning. Then he smiled to himself. He should have known better. Charlotte was always in her office bright and early, no matter what. She was a dedicated career girl.

He took a moment to study her now. She seemed completely engrossed in the papers in front of her. Her long blonde hair was piled up on top of her head, exposing the creamy length of her neck. As usual she was dressed in a smart, businesslike black trouser suit, with a white blouse open at the neck. She had a great figure—he allowed himself to remember her soft curves and the long, shapely legs and found himself wanting her all over again. Not a good start, he warned himself with annoyance. He was going to have to play this very carefully.

She glanced up and their eyes collided briefly. Only the pallor of her skin and the faint shadows under her green eyes gave away the fact that she wasn't entirely at ease. She gave him a brief smile then returned her attention to her work.

Charlotte cursed herself as she fixed her eyes on her

papers. Maybe she shouldn't have smiled? She had been telling herself all morning that she should just act like normal—but what was normal? She couldn't seem to remember how she usually behaved around Jordan. It was all muddled up in her mind now with memories of red-hot passion last night. Concentrate on work, she told herself fiercely.

At least her designs were taking good shape, she thought, running a critical eye over them. Sometimes it seemed as if she did her best work when she was under duress—maybe because she used work like an escape valve. When she entered her world of interior design she could shut the door on everything and everyone else. Jordan was a bit like that as well; they had remarked long ago that when it came to work they were remarkably similar, both totally dedicated. Which was probably the reason they had worked so well together lately.

Had she jeopardised that last night? Right at this moment Charlotte doubted very much that she could even pretend to be relaxed around him again.

The door of her office opened and she was aware of his dark eyes raking over her even before she glanced up. She held herself very straight, as if she was completely at ease and in control of the situation, and gave him a brief smile. 'Hi, Jordan. You're late—the accountant will be in soon and we have those figures to sort out.' She was pleased at how confident she sounded.

'Of course I'm late.' He put down his briefcase and came around to perch on the edge of her desk.

Couldn't he just use the seat opposite like any other normal person? Charlotte wondered nervously. She felt at enough of a disadvantage this morning without him looming over her like some kind of bird of prey.

'Some feisty young woman kept me very busy last night.' His voice was softly teasing.

She felt her skin glow with vivid colour.

There was a moment's silence, a moment where he waited for her to say something. When she didn't his eyes moved with thorough gentleness over her upturned face, taking in the colour on her high cheekbones, the softness of her lips. 'Why did you rush off like that this morning?' he asked.

She leaned further back in her chair, trying to feign an indifference that she just didn't feel. 'Last night was... pleasant, Jordan—'

'Yes, it was,' Jordan agreed, a wry gleam in his eyes. 'Very pleasant.'

'But we've got to work together and I don't think we should complicate things.'

'Who said anything about complicating things?' Jordan shrugged. 'I'm all for keeping things simple.'

She nodded. 'Of course.' She had never for one moment thought that he would read anything serious into last night. 'Look, I'll be honest with you, I'm feeling a bit awkward.' She tried desperately to hold his gaze but failed miserably and had to look away. 'I'm hoping we can put this...incident behind us and forget about it, go back to the way things used to be.'

Jordan reached out a hand and tipped her chin upwards so that she was forced to meet his eyes. 'Do you feel guilty about last night because you are still in love with David?' He asked the question quietly.

The question and the touch of his hand against her skin brought a very heated response coursing through her veins. 'I don't think that's any of your business, Jordan,' she snapped, pulling away from him.

He shrugged. 'Well, if you are still holding a torch for David, you're making a big mistake. The guy is a loser.'

'And I really don't need your analysis of David, thank

you. You're hardly a model of perfection where women are concerned yourself.'

Jordan smiled at that. 'You weren't complaining last night,' he said teasingly and watched the even brighter flare of colour in her cheeks.

'You see! This is exactly why last night was such a mistake,' she spluttered indignantly. 'I can't have you reminding me about it every two minutes we have to work together.'

'I'm not reminding you about it every two minutes; we were discussing the implications of last night before moving on to the day's work, like a couple of grown-ups—remember?'

'Don't get smart with me, Jordan. There are no implications from last night; it was just two people enjoying a bit of light-hearted fun. So let's just forget about it and move on. OK?'

'Fine with me.' Jordan shrugged.

'Good.' She picked up some papers that were sitting beside her. 'Those are for you; they are the estimates for the soft furnishings.'

'Great, thanks.' His voice was dry. 'I'll look through them and get back to you.'

'Good idea.'

'And I've got something for you.' He opened his briefcase. She thought he was going to pass her some papers that he wanted her to look at. Instead he took out a folded black lacy bra and put it on her desk. 'It was on the floor in the lounge.'

Mortified beyond belief, Charlotte grabbed it and stuck it in the top drawer of her desk. 'What are you thinking of?' she said shakily, glancing around through the glass walls to see if any of her co-workers had noticed. Her office made her feel a bit like she worked in a goldfish bowl—everyone could see what she was doing.

'Well, I was thinking that you might just be missing your bra,' he said with a smile.

'I've got to work here, Jordan! I don't want everyone knowing that I've had a moment's insanity with the boss.'

'Charlotte, they'd have to have bionic vision to see what that tiny scrap of material is,' he said with a shake of his head. 'Relax, for heaven's sake.' Before she realised his intention he reached out and tipped her chin up so that she was forced to meet his eyes.

'And as moments of insanity go it was very, very pleasant,' he murmured huskily, his eyes moving towards her lips.

Then he released her and walked out of her office. Her heart was thumping. She felt sick inside with the knowledge that she had just handled that situation appallingly. Maybe she should just have laughed the whole thing off instead of acting so uptight?

Breathing deeply to release the tension inside, Charlotte tried very hard to think straight. But her mind was a jumbled mess of words and feelings she couldn't get a handle on. In desperation she reached for the phone and dialled her sister's number.

The answering machine came on and she was just about to hang up in complete frustration when Jennifer answered, sounding a bit breathless.

'Oh, hi, sis. Sorry, I was just attending to Matilda here. She won't stop crying.'

In the background Charlotte could hear her four-week-old niece giving full vent to her lungs. 'Sorry, I've obviously caught you at a bad time. I'll ring back later.'

'No, no, it's OK,' Jennifer assured her hastily. 'What's the matter?'

Charlotte smiled to herself. Jennifer was her younger sister by five years but they were very close. 'You know me so well,' she murmured.

'I know that tone in your voice, if that's what you mean.' Jennifer was shushing her baby and Charlotte could hear her picking her up, could imagine the scene as she wedged a phone on one shoulder whilst holding a wriggling infant on the other.

'I don't know what's the matter with me. I'm not coping with anything at the moment, and my emotions are all over the place.'

'Well, I think that's pretty normal given the circumstances with you and David. You have been dating him for a long time; you're bound to be upset. You should have taken time off work—'

'Jen, I did something terrible last night.' She cut across her sister, swiftly needing to unburden herself. 'I slept with Jordan.'

There was a deathly silence at the other end of the phone. Even Matilda had gone quiet.

'Crikey, Charlie!'

'I know!' Charlotte flicked a glance through the glass partition and saw Jordan's secretary laughing with him. He looked incredibly relaxed and for some reason that made Charlotte feel even more on edge. 'I don't know what happened! One moment I was going to have coffee with him and the next we were in bed.'

Jennifer laughed.

'It's not funny.'

'No, but it's not that terrible either! To be honest, I've always secretly thought that Jordan would be perfect for you. Dad thinks so too. In fact he was saying not so long ago how well you two work together now and what a blessing he has you both at the business. And Jordan is so nice and so good-looking—'

'Oh, come on!' Charlotte cut in drily. 'Don't start taking artistic licence. The only thing Dad would say is that

Jordan makes lots of money for the company. Dad is a businessman first and foremost.'

'No, he's not. He's a big softie really, and he'll be pleased you're having a relationship with Jordan.'

'We're not having a relationship—it was sex!'

'Well, a relationship has to start somewhere. Why not in bed? At least you've sampled the goods and found them in working order.' Jennifer giggled. 'I'm so pleased. If nothing else, you needed someone to take your mind off David.'

Jordan had certainly done that, Charlotte thought wryly.

'Listen, why don't the two of you come for Sunday dinner?' Jennifer said excitedly.

'I don't think you've been listening to me, Jen. We're not dating. In fact, we're barely being civil to each other this morning. And besides, you know what he's like where women are concerned—I'll be just another notch on his bedpost.'

'Not necessarily; you could be special.'

'And the world could be flat,' Charlotte drawled. 'Anyway, it's too close for comfort. I've got to work with the guy and I don't want the complications; I've enough problems. I don't know what the hell possessed me.'

'I do—he's gorgeous!' Jennifer giggled again. 'All right, well, you just come for dinner then. I'd better go. Madam here has just been sick down my blouse. See you Sunday.'

'See you Sunday.' Charlotte was speaking to a dead phone line now. She supposed she shouldn't be surprised that Jennifer would be pro-Jordan. She'd been singing his praises since he had joined the company, and her husband, Steve, had got very friendly with him. Even though they lived just outside London in quite a rural area, Jordan was often over at their house. In fact it was through her sister that Charlotte got to hear snippets of information about Jordan's girlfriends.

It was a wonder Jennifer didn't know about the fact he had once had a daughter. But she definitely didn't, otherwise Charlotte would have heard about it. Obviously it was just too painful a subject for Jordan to talk about, which was understandable.

She glanced down at the designs in front of her, but her mind was flicking over Jennifer's words.

I've always secretly thought that Jordan would be perfect for you. Dad thinks so too.

Where had that come from? Jennifer had never said that to her before. And as for her father, he would think anyone was good for her as long as it wasn't David. He really disliked David, and that was before he had heard of their break-up.

But Jen was wrong. Romantically speaking, Jordan wasn't her type. He was too sure of himself, arrogant even. But then she remembered last night and the way he had made her laugh at dinner…the way he had looked so raw when he had spoken of his little girl…the way he had kissed the inside of her wrist… Why had that kiss been so erotic? she wondered. She had never thought of the wrist being an erogenous zone before.

She frowned. All right, maybe last night Jordan had sort of grown on her a bit. But not romantically, definitely not romantically; Jennifer was wrong about that. The sex had been wonderful though.

Charlotte scored a line through the piece of paper in front of her. She had to work with the guy, she told herself fiercely. Remembering things like that wasn't helpful.

She looked over at him again; he was signing something now and he gave Laura a boyish smile that for some reason had a funny effect on Charlotte's loins. He *was* basically a nice man. Obviously he had loved his wife, and his little girl. Whatever was going on in his life now, he'd certainly been through a tough time in the past.

Maybe she should apologise for being a bit sharp this morning. They had both enjoyed last night. She should have acted in a more mature way about it all.

She watched as Laura left his office. He was talking to someone on the phone now. If she was going to apologise, now was probably the time to go over, whilst his secretary was out. She didn't want the whole building knowing that she was Jordan's latest conquest. That would be too humiliating.

Before her courage could desert her she got up and went across to his office. They never knocked on each other's doors, so Charlotte didn't think twice about just walking in on him. He was sitting with his back to her, having swivelled around in his leather chair, and he was still talking on the phone.

'We went out for dinner,' he was saying. 'Then I invited her back to my place for coffee.' He laughed, a deep, husky, teasing kind of laugh. 'OK, what can I say? I'm weak, yeah…that's right, I got sidetracked. Not one of my better moves. But it was very enjoyable.'

Charlotte's blood started to freeze in her veins as she realised he was talking about her.

Her first instinct was to get out of the room before he saw that she was there. She certainly wasn't going to apologise to him now. Hurriedly she started to back away, closing the door behind her with a quiet click. How dared he? she thought as she stormed back to her office. Not one of his better moves, indeed! He could say that again!

She sat back down at her desk and glared at the back of his head through the plate glass. How dared he discuss her like that…and who had he been talking to? She hoped it wasn't someone they worked with—if this got out in the office everyone would be gossiping about her.

She burned with the indignity of it all. She had always been an intensely private person. And she had always prided herself on being in control of her emotions. Now her personal life was being bandied around for all and sundry to know, and she certainly wasn't in control of her emotions because at this moment she really thought she hated Jordan Lynch.

His chair swivelled around suddenly and their eyes locked through the glass. Hers simmered with intense anger, his were coolly unperturbed.

Swiftly she lowered her head and returned her attention to her work. That was it; she would have nothing more to do with Jordan Lynch, she told herself fiercely.

CHAPTER THREE

IT WAS Sunday afternoon, the sky was a clear blue but the breeze that stirred the trees, sending showers of cherry blossom fluttering onto the front lawns, was ice-cold. It felt more like March than the first day of May, Charlotte thought as she pulled up outside the tall Victorian detached house where Jennifer and Steven lived.

She parked her car on the road and walked into the driveway past her sister's people carrier, Steve's convertible and Harriet's bicycle, which had been abandoned at right angles by the front door in a strategically placed booby trap.

Smiling to herself, Charlotte stepped over it and in through the front door, which had been left ajar.

The first thing that hit her was the smell of roast beef wafting through from the kitchen; the second was the discordant sound of Harriet practising her scales on the piano in the lounge.

'Hello,' Charlotte called out. Immediately the playing stopped and her six-year-old niece came flying out, feet thundering on the polished wooden floors, blonde pigtails bouncing as she flung herself at Charlotte like a whirling dervish.

'Auntie Charlie!' she screeched with delight as Charlotte picked her up and whirled her around. 'Guess what…guess what?'

'What?' Charlotte hugged her tight and then put her down.

'Uncle Jordan is here as well.'

'Oh.' The moment of happiness inside Charlotte faded

as she looked up and saw Jordan framed in the kitchen doorway, watching the welcome she had received. Charlotte was used to seeing Jordan dressed in suits but today he was wearing jeans and an open-necked blue shirt. The casual look suited him, made him look younger than his thirty-eight years, and even sexier than usual, if that was possible. She dragged her gaze away from him, annoyed for thinking along those lines.

'Hello, Jordan.' She was aware that her voice was very cool, but she couldn't help it. She had been looking forward to a relaxing dinner with her family, away from her problems, especially the problem of Jordan. 'What are you doing here?' Even as she asked the question she knew the answer.

'Jennifer invited me over for lunch.'

She hoped to high heaven he didn't think she'd put Jen up to it! Jordan Lynch didn't need his ego boosting any further—it was already off the scale.

'That was nice of her.' There was a definite edge to Charlotte's tone now.

He smiled, totally unperturbed. 'Yes, I thought so too.'

Charlotte took off her beige suede jacket and slung it over the end of the banisters. She was going to kill her sister.

'Where is Jen?'

'On the phone, trying to dig Steve out of the golf club. He went for a quick game and apparently should have been home over an hour ago.'

Charlotte smiled. That sounded like Steve. 'I'm surprised you didn't join him.'

Jordan shrugged. 'I had to go into the office today to sort out some paperwork.'

For the first time Charlotte realised just how much extra work Jordan had on his desk with her father staying on in France all this time. 'If you need some help with paperwork I don't mind giving you a hand,' she offered impulsively. 'I know I'm more on the design side than office management, but I can do both. I did run my own business once.'

'Yes, I know.' He smiled at her. 'Thanks, I'll bear that in mind.'

Something about the way he smiled at her made her go hot inside. Hurriedly she glanced away. Then, catching her niece's eye, she remembered she had some sweets for her in her jacket pocket. She took them out and passed them to the little girl.

'Thanks!' Harriet's eyes lit up. 'These are my favourites. And look what Uncle Jordan brought.' She raced into the lounge and came back with a rag doll in one hand and a teddy in the other. 'This is for me, and this…' she brandished the teddy '…is for Matilda.'

'How lovely.' Charlotte smiled. 'I hope you said a big thank-you to Uncle Jordan.'

Harriet nodded. 'He's a lovely uncle.' She said the words with a seriousness that sounded very grown-up for a six-year-old.

Charlotte laughed and glanced over at Jordan with amusement.

'It's official, I'm a lovely uncle.' He nodded, humour also sparkling in his dark eyes. 'Even if it is only an honorary title.'

Maybe he was a bit of a rat when it came to love, but you couldn't help but like the guy, Charlotte thought. 'Well, it was very kind of you.'

As she made to follow him into the kitchen she noticed the gleam of male interest that took in her close-fitting beige leather trousers and cream jumper. It was as if he could see straight through to the scanty underwear beneath and, shockingly, it made her body leap in a response that was purely sexual as she remembered the wild passion they had shared on Thursday night.

Instantly she was annoyed with herself, and annoyed with him for looking at her like that. Would their night together never be forgotten? She had the horrible feeling that it was going to haunt the rest of their working relationship. Remembering the way he had talked about her on the phone, she cringed inwardly. She'd been such a fool.

Matilda was in her carry-cot by the French doors, and, glad of the diversion, Charlotte went across to peep into the lacy crib. She expected the baby to be asleep, she was so quiet, and got quite a surprise when Matilda turned big blue eyes up at her and seemed to smile.

'Hello, darling,' Charlotte cooed and touched one of the tiny hands that rested on the counterpane. 'Hello.'

Jennifer was so lucky, Charlotte thought, so incredibly lucky to have two such gorgeous children.

'Would you like a glass of wine?' Jordan asked from the other end of the kitchen. 'I opened a bottle of Chablis a little while ago.'

'Thanks.' Charlotte glanced down the modern white kitchen. He seemed very much at home here, she thought as she watched him open up the fridge and pour her the wine.

'Won't be a minute, Charlotte,' Jennifer called down the stairs. 'They are sending search parties out to find Steve at the golf club—he's going to be dead meat when he gets home.'

Charlotte laughed. 'Leave him alone, you bully,' she called back.

'No chance. Harriet, I can't hear you practising your scales.'

The little girl pulled a face at her mother's words but

dutifully disappeared back towards the lounge to resume her discordant serenade.

'Married bliss, eh?' Jordan smiled as he brought her drink over and put it down on the table next to her. She almost smiled back at him, and then stopped herself. She really was going to have to keep a cool distance from Jordan. OK, he had notched her up on his bedpost, but he needn't think she was a pushover.

'I hope you don't think that I asked Jen to invite you here today,' she told him bluntly as she sat down. 'Because I didn't.'

'The thought hadn't occurred to me. I'm often here.'

'So I believe.'

He took out one of the wrought-iron chairs from the kitchen table and put it down to sit facing her.

'Can we go back to being friends, Charlie?' he asked quietly.

She noticed how his knees were almost touching hers. Her eyes rested on his hands, which were large and capable-looking. She remembered how they had felt against her body, caressing her to a fever pitch of desire. Remembered how she had writhed and moaned and kissed him with a hunger that she had never known before.

'Charlie?' he prompted.

'Of course,' she replied quickly.

She looked at him and her eyes shimmered intensely green. But had they ever been just friends? she wondered suddenly. She had always been so acutely aware of him, always intensely careful to keep a distance. And with good reason, she realised now.

Charlotte's words didn't convince Jordan. It was as if she had just rolled down steel shutters on herself.

'You could have fooled me,' he said steadily. 'Since our evening together there's an occasional chill coming off you that feels as if it could be rolling in from Antarctica.'

'Is there?' She frowned. 'Well, I'm sorry if that's the case. I really don't want to jeopardise our working relationship.'

She noticed how his lips twisted drily at those words. 'No, neither do I.' He leaned back in his chair. 'We need to stick together, Charlie, because we have a lot of…stuff to get through over the next few weeks.'

'You mean with Dad being away and it being so busy in the office?'

'Sort of…' Jordan hesitated. 'I think you should know that I offered to buy your father's share of the business from him a while ago.'

Instantly Charlotte felt apprehensive. Her father was her only safety barrier between herself and Jordan. And after their night together she needed that protection more than ever.

He watched her reaction carefully as he spoke and saw the concern in her eyes. 'He turned down my offer.'

'Oh…' There was relief in her look now. 'Well, you can't blame him, Jordan. The business has been in our family for two generations.'

'And family is very important to the McCanns.'

'Yes.' She shrugged. 'There's nothing wrong with that, is there?'

'No, and I can understand your sentiments. Obviously you want to take over a share of the running of the company one day, and so you should. You've worked very hard to make the interior-design division a success.'

'Why do I sense that the word ''but'' is going to creep into this?' Charlotte reached for her glass of wine.

'I don't think your father can afford to turn down my offer,' Jordan said bluntly.

'Why ever not?' She laughed at the absurdity of that remark. 'He's a wealthy man. He can afford to do whatever he likes.'

Jordan looked thoughtful. 'But it isn't only down to money. He has become forgetful and his business judgement isn't as sharp as it has been in the past. I know he lost a lot of money on shares last year and…' He hesitated and lowered his voice. 'I really haven't wanted to tell you this, Charlotte, but I feel I must. The auditors did a spot check and there is a substantial amount of money missing from the company accounts.'

It took a moment for what he was saying to sink in. 'Are you saying my father is stealing from the company?' Her words trembled alarmingly.

'I didn't say that.'

'You might as well have!' She cut across him. 'My father is an honourable man—how can you suggest such a thing?' She glared at him.

'I'm just being honest with you, so there's no point being angry.' Jordan's voice was calm. 'If it makes you feel any better, I think your father is innocent and that Ruth is the culprit. I have a feeling she has taken the money without your father's knowledge.'

'This is preposterous.' Charlotte shook her head. 'Why would Ruth take money from the company?'

'I don't know. But I got a phone call from her last week and she was very agitated. At first I couldn't make out what she was talking about. She was babbling on about the accounts and money but before she could explain she got cut off.'

Charlotte stared at him in distress. And a prickle of unease crept in to disturb her certainty. Her father had only been married to Ruth for two years and Charlotte had worried about the match at first, but her only concern had been their age difference. Her father was nearly sixty; Ruth was forty-six. However, they seemed so ideally happy together that Charlotte had stopped thinking about age as an issue at all. And she had grown extremely fond of Ruth. 'I can't imagine for one moment that Ruth would dip into company funds.'

'Well, I've given the matter serious thought since the phone call,' Jordan said. 'And Ruth used to work in the accounts department, didn't she?'

Charlotte nodded.

'So she knows her way around the systems very well.'

'I still can't believe she would do such a thing,' Charlotte said firmly. 'Apart from anything else, Dad is a wealthy man. She wouldn't need to do it.'

'Well, the money is definitely missing. And, reading between the lines, that's how it looks to me—'

'There must be something more to this, something we don't know.' Charlotte's voice was emphatic.

'Don't you think it speaks volumes that they haven't come back from France?' he asked quietly. 'And since discovering the money has gone, I haven't been able to make contact with them.'

Charlotte had to admit that was a bit odd. Her father was such a workaholic; he loved the office. But she had thought that Ruth was making him take an extra-long break. In fact she had even secretly applauded Ruth for the action, because her father had looked so tired before he left. But now…

'How much money are we talking about?' she asked curiously.

'It's not the amount of money that's the problem, it's the implication. These are serious charges; if they were to be made public the scandal could ruin the good reputation of the business. I'm sorry, Charlie…really I am.' He reached to touch her but she flinched away.

Then, unable to bear his close proximity a moment longer, she got up from her chair to stand with her back to him, staring out of the windows.

'Look, the situation can be salvaged, but it will have to

be done fast. If your father can't afford to pay the money back, then we can come to an agreement. I can afford to pay the debt and in return your father can transfer the equivalent shares in the business over to me, giving me overall control of the company.'

The calm, businesslike words made a wave of anger rise in Charlotte. He had it all sorted out in his mind by the sound of it. 'How convenient for you,' she murmured. 'You've wanted control of the business from the moment you walked in, haven't you?'

'That's not fair, Charlie.'

'But it's true.' She stared sightlessly at the tulips that danced in the breeze at the end of the garden. 'You're ambitious…and you like power.'

When he didn't answer she turned around to look at him. He got up from his chair and came towards her. 'There is nothing wrong with being ambitious,' he said softly. 'You are too, otherwise you wouldn't be so good at your job.'

When she didn't reply he stepped closer. 'You are not so different from me, Charlotte McCann.'

'I think we are very different,' she replied steadily. 'I'm worried about my father. Whilst you are worrying about getting control of the business.'

'I'm worried about the future of the business and that's a different thing. I told you this affects us all and it could be serious.' He looked very cold now and very hard. 'And I'll have to be honest with you, Charlotte. Your father hasn't been his usual self these last six months. And I can't have a business partner that I can't rely on.'

She flinched at that. Jordan Lynch was a businessman first and foremost, she thought. The business side of her could see exactly where he was coming from. But the emotional side, the side that remembered that he had been her father's friend, was having severe difficulty in accepting those words.

'But you will allow time to sort this out, Jordan—if Ruth has taken the money you will give them time to pay it back?'

Jordan didn't answer her straight away and the serious look in his eyes made her heart jump. 'I don't think I can. I need control of the company now.'

She felt sick suddenly.

'And I'll need your help.' Jordan's voice was decisive. 'I can't contact your father on his mobile phone and I don't know exactly where he is in France. You are going to have to help me track him down, perhaps speak to him for me. Because we can't go on like this.'

Charlotte felt her heart thumping against her breast so forcefully that it was painful. 'I'm sure this is all just some terrible mistake,' she murmured brokenly.

Jordan came closer to her. 'But you'll help me to sort it out?'

She hesitated for a second and then nodded.

'Thanks. Try not to worry too much about it.' The softness of his voice and the closeness of his body were sending very conflicting signals through her now. He had been so cold and businesslike when he had spoken about her father, and that made her angry, but weaving its way insidiously through that anger was the memory of how tenderly and passionately he had held her the other night and it made her want to fold into his arms. She despised herself for the momentary weakness and yet perversely the feeling lingered.

There was the sound of footsteps on the stairs and Jordan reached out a hand and took hold of her arm. 'Don't mention any of this to Jennifer,' he told her. 'I know you tell each other everything, but this is one thing you need to keep to yourself. She's just had a baby, and Steve is already a bit worried about her.'

'I know that.' Charlotte frowned. She was well aware of the fact that Jen had enough to cope with. She was just surprised that Jordan had the sensitivity to realise it.

When Jennifer came through the doorway Charlotte could tell instantly that she flew to all the wrong conclusions when she saw them standing so closely together. Her face lit up in a brilliant smile that shone from her gentle blue eyes.

'Hi, sis; did you find Steve eventually?' Charlotte moved hastily away from Jordan and went to kiss her sister on the cheek.

Jennifer and Charlotte were not unalike; they both had the same blonde hair that was inclined to curliness, only Jennifer's was cut in a short style that suited her delicate features. She'd lost a bit of weight, Charlotte noticed, because she was already back in the jeans she had been wearing before becoming pregnant. That wasn't so good. They had to keep an eye on Jennifer because she had suffered from anorexia as a teenager and she was still prone to bouts of worrying about her weight. But they never talked too much about that—she had recovered and they wanted to keep it that way.

'Yes, he's on his way home in a taxi.' Jennifer's eyes darted from her to Jordan speculatively. 'You two seemed very deep in conversation. Everything all right?'

'Oh, yes, fine.' Charlotte lied airily.

'Great.' Jennifer gave a satisfied smile and suddenly Charlotte had the distinct impression that Steve's disappearance to the golf club and her non-appearance for so long had all been an elaborate charade to throw them together. And obviously Jen believed it had worked.

'Right, well, I'll see to dinner. Steve will be here in a minute and he'll be starving.'

'I'll give you a hand,' Charlotte said, following her sister to the other end of the kitchen.

'So how are things at the office?' Jen asked conversationally as she took an enormous roast of beef out of the oven.

'Busy as usual.' Jordan was the one to answer.

'I'm surprised Dad has stayed away so long. I reckon Ruth must be good for him. Usually he'd be frothing at the mouth to get back to his desk.'

Half an hour ago Charlotte would have laughed and agreed. Now her eyes met with Jordan's and she felt the weight of what he had just told her press down on her.

They were saved from having to reply to that because Matilda started to cry.

As Jennifer was busy seeing to the vegetables and Charlotte was making the gravy, Jordan stood up. 'Would you like me to see to her?' he asked.

'If you wouldn't mind?' Jen nodded.

'I'll come through in a minute,' Charlotte told him, wondering if he could cope, but she needn't have worried. When she glanced down the room she saw that he was cradling the child on his shoulder, gently rubbing her back.

'There, there, honey, that's a big noise for a little girl, isn't it?' he murmured.

And this was the same man who had been so cold and businesslike just a few moments ago? Charlotte thought. He seemed so warmly at ease now and he was so good with the baby. Considering Matilda was so tiny and fragile against the large hands that held her, he didn't seem the slightest bit awkward. After a moment she gave a little hiccup and the crying stopped.

'That's better,' Jordan soothed, and went to put her back down again. A few minutes later they could hear him talking to Harriet as she banged away on the keyboard.

'Isn't he wonderful?' Jen grinned at Charlotte.

She wouldn't think he was so wonderful if she knew what he had just been saying about their dad, Charlotte thought grimly. 'I think you can leave the matchmaking bit out, Jen,' she said.

But Jennifer was undeterred. 'Bet you're glad I invited him now, aren't you?' she said smugly. 'I can see how things are between you two. If I'd waited a couple more seconds you'd have been in a passionate clinch. Wait until Dad hears—he'll be thrilled.'

Charlotte wanted to say that it wasn't how it looked, but refrained in case Jen started to question her too deeply. 'Have you heard anything from Dad?' she asked casually instead.

'No. I really miss him, Charlie. I can't even reach him on his cell-phone because it's switched off.' She pulled a face. 'I hate not being able to talk to him; ridiculous, isn't it…?' She trailed off and smiled.

They heard the slam of the front door and Steve's voice shouting that he was home.

'About time too,' Jen called back and then grinned at Charlotte.

'You're not cross with him at all,' Charlotte said, glad that the subject was changed. 'And if you are thinking of starting a career in matchmaking I'd give it a miss, if I were you. You're lousy at it. For the record, Jordan and I are just good friends.'

'That's what I used to say about Steve.'

There wasn't much time to talk after that. Charlotte busied herself assisting with the dinner, glad to have something to help take her mind off her father. But once they were seated at the dining table she started to think about him again. And, delicious as the food was, it seemed to stick in her throat.

She kept remembering other happy occasions when they had sat at this table with her father.

Steve was talking about his engineering business, but Charlotte was thinking that they had been sitting here when their father had announced he was getting married again.

'I've met the woman I want to spend the rest of my life with,' he had announced. It had been such an emotional and happy moment and they had all really wanted this marriage to work out for him.

Jordan had to be wrong about Ruth, he just had to be, she thought fiercely.

As if he could read her thoughts Jordan's eyes locked with hers across the table. He seemed to be watching her very intently.

Suddenly she remembered the way he had questioned her about her father when they were out for dinner. Was that why he had asked her out in the first place? If so, it made what had happened later even more excruciatingly hard to think about without breaking into a cold sweat.

'You're very quiet, Charlie,' Jennifer remarked suddenly.

'Am I?' Conscious of everyone's eyes suddenly on her, Charlotte felt herself colouring guiltily. 'Sorry, I was just relaxing.'

'Charlotte's been working far too hard,' Jordan cut in. 'You're probably tired, aren't you, Charlie.'

'Probably.' Charlotte glared at him; she could speak for herself.

Jennifer shook her head. 'Honestly, sis, you're just like Dad where that business is concerned. I know it's very important to you, but you need to let up—take advantage of the fact you've got Jordan at the helm now and relax a bit.'

Charlotte studiously avoided Jordan's eyes. 'Yes, you're right,' she murmured.

Steve lifted the wine bottle and made to refill her glass.

'Oh, I can't have another drink, Steve, I'm driving.' She hurriedly put her hand over the glass.

'I'll drive you home, Charlotte.' Jordan's voice was firm, making more like a command than an offer.

After a moment's hesitation she lifted her hand. She needed to talk some more to Jordan about the situation anyway, so she might as well let him drop her home, she thought resignedly.

The light was fading outside and Jennifer lit the candles on the table.

'Anyone want coffee?' Steve asked, standing up.

'Not for me, thanks.' Jordan smiled. 'But I'll give you a hand to stack the dishwasher.' He waved away Jennifer's objections as he got to his feet. 'It's the least I can do after such a lovely meal.'

'You OK?' Jennifer asked Charlotte as soon as they were left alone.

'Yes, fine.' Charlotte smiled and then hastily got to her feet. She had to get away before her sister started probing further. Jennifer knew her too well not to realise something was wrong.

'Excuse me a moment,' she said.

Escaping into the downstairs bathroom, she flicked on the overhead light and leaned back against the door. Her reflection stared back at her from three walls, her eyes looked too big for the delicate, heart-shaped face and her skin was very pale. She realised that the shock of what Jordan had told her was only just starting to sink in fully. Splashing her face with cold water, she reapplied her lipstick and tried to gather herself together. There would be a reasonable explanation for why the money was missing from the business, and her father would be fine. But she would like to speak to him before Jordan did. It might be easier.

The best thing she could do now was to make an excuse

and leave before her sister realised something was wrong. Having come to that decision, she felt a bit better.

She could hear voices coming from the kitchen as she walked back out into the hall. Jordan was asking Jennifer if she'd heard from her father recently.

'No. I was saying earlier to Charlotte, I miss him, but at least he must be having a great time.'

'The south of France is very beautiful. I used to live there, you know, and I still have a place not far from St Tropez. As a matter of fact, I was the one who recommended them to that area. I actually offered my villa to Simon, but Ruth said they were just going to do a bit of touring, that she had already booked all the accommodation.'

'Yes, I think Ruth had a fair idea of where she wanted to go. When they were down there late last year she just fell in love with the place.'

Charlotte stood in the doorway and took in the scene. It all looked very cosy. Jordan and Steve were doing the dishes. Jennifer was sitting at the table with Matilda on her knee.

'So where do you think Ruth and your father will have gravitated to?'

The question was asked with expert ease. If she hadn't known better she would have thought that Jordan was just a lovely person making polite conversation. But she did know better, and the white heat of panic flooded through her.

'Well, the last thing Dad said to me was—'

'I'm sorry to break up the party,' Charlotte cut across her sister swiftly, 'but Jordan and I are going to have to leave now.'

They all looked around at her.

'But it's still only early!' Jennifer said.

'I'm sorry, Jen, but I've got work to do before to-morrow.'

'Work again.' Jennifer rolled her eyes. 'It's Sunday eve-ning!' She turned back to Jordan. 'Tell Charlotte she has to have the night off, Jordan,' she said with a smile. 'Re-mind her who is the boss, for heaven's sake.'

Jordan looked over Jennifer's head and met Charlotte's steady cool gaze. 'I'm the boss—no work tonight, Charlie,' he complied, his voice authoritative. Then he grinned, and lowered his voice huskily. 'What you need is an early night.'

The implied innuendo hung heavily and embarrassingly in the air.

'Oh, I see,' Jennifer giggled. 'You should have said so before! In that case I'll let you two lovebirds go home.'

Charlotte felt angry at how Jordan had turned that around, but somehow she managed to smile tightly. Luck-ily her sister just seemed to think she was self-conscious.

'Anyway, we won't detain you,' Jen said, standing up and following her out to the hallway as she turned away.

As Charlotte reached for her jacket on the banister Jor-dan took it from her and helped her into it. The touch of his hands brushing against her body made her temperature rise even more. She wanted to push him away but couldn't because both her sister and Steve were standing watching them.

'Oh, I keep forgetting to tell you, Charlie,' Jennifer said suddenly. 'Steve and I have asked Jordan to be Matilda's godfather and he's agreed. So you'll both be godparents—isn't that lovely? And sort of romantic in a way with you two…getting on so well.'

'Lovely.' Charlotte could hardly find her breath. 'But we're not—'

'Sure what to buy as a christening gift,' Jordan cut in

firmly and the hand that was resting on her shoulder tightened imperceptibly.

'Oh, we've got loads of time to talk about that,' Jennifer said happily. 'It's not until the beginning of June. Hopefully Dad and Ruth will be back by then. You do think they will be, don't you?'

'Oh, yes,' Jordan said briskly. 'It's ages away.'

'It's to be hoped we have loads of time,' Steve said with a grin as he put an arm around his wife. 'We still haven't agreed on a real name for Matilda here.'

'I'd stick with Matilda if I were you. It's kind of grown on me,' Jordan said easily.

'Oh, no.' Steve shook his head. 'Matilda was just a stopgap so we weren't calling her "the baby" all the time. She's going to be Estelle, after my mother.'

'I think not.' Jennifer grinned.

Charlotte tried to pull away from Jordan but the hand on her shoulder was too strong.

'Well, thanks again for a lovely dinner.' He smiled and reached to kiss Jennifer on the cheek. Then looked down at the sleeping baby in her arms. 'Whatever you call her, she's a beautiful baby.'

The front door opened, letting in a blast of unseasonably cold night air.

'Goodnight, Steve…Jen.' Charlotte kissed them. 'Thank you for a lovely evening.'

She walked out of the door with Jordan's hand still on her shoulder.

'Bye, Uncle Jordan…bye, Auntie Charlie.' Harriet's small voice drifted to them and they turned to wave to her.

For a moment the family were silhouetted against the warmth of the hall. Then the door closed and they were alone.

CHAPTER FOUR

'WAS that remark really necessary?' Charlotte's voice was as cold as the weather.

'What remark?' Jordan asked with a grin as he moved to walk around to the driver's side of his sports car.

'I'm going to take my own car home,' she said, glaring at him across the machine's roof. 'I didn't touch that glass of wine Steve gave me, so I'm perfectly OK to drive. And I don't think we should talk until I've had time to think about things.'

'Just get in, Charlotte,' he said curtly. 'It's too damn cold for histrionics.'

'Histrionics?' Charlotte wanted to throw something at him. She had never felt a need to vent her anger physically before but it was boiling up inside her now.

He unlocked his car and got in and she was left standing on the pavement with enough heat coming off her to roast the night air.

The engine of the car started with a powerful purr, then the electric window wound down. 'Are you going to stand there freezing, or are you getting in? Harriet is watching you from an upstairs window.'

Charlotte glanced around and saw the little girl framed in her bedroom window. She was still waving. Charlotte waved back and then, gritting her teeth, got into the car.

It was already warm inside and it smelt of leather and Jordan's cologne, a strange, clean, cool kind of mixture that for some reason made her feel even more on edge.

As soon as her seat belt clicked into place he pulled out into the road.

'Are you going to tell me why there is steam coming out of your ears?' he enquired with maddening equanimity.

'I think you are a bit of a charlatan.' She glared across at him. 'You told me not to worry Jen with this business about Dad, and then I hear you quizzing her in the kitchen.'

'I wasn't quizzing her.'

'You could have fooled me,' she said derisively. 'Heard anything from your father yet, Jen?' She mimicked his friendly, bantering question. 'Know where he is so I can send the fraud squad around? Very friendly.'

He flicked an amused glance over at her. 'I was just making conversation.'

'You should have been a politician, Jordan Lynch,' she muttered. 'They are good at kissing babies and pretending to have a heart too.'

'Have you quite finished?'

'And you were filling Jen's head full of nonsense about us,' she continued heatedly. 'That was an outrageously suggestive remark about us having an early night, totally over the top.'

'It got us out of there, didn't it? And as excuses go I thought it was quite believable,' he said with a grin and glanced over at her. 'Well, it's not as if we haven't spent the night together before, is it?'

'Will you just forget about that?' She glared at him. 'That was a mistake.'

'Lighten up, Charlie; we both enjoyed the other night and you know it.'

The light-hearted arrogance fuelled the temper inside her even further. 'Let me tell you,' she blustered, 'I'd rather sleep with...with...with the devil himself than sleep with you again. I wouldn't want you to touch me.'

Jordan glanced over at her with a wry expression in his eyes, but he said nothing.

As soon as Charlotte made that remark she knew she had just gone a step too far. The rage that had suddenly gripped her was now fading as fast as it had appeared. And she realised that a lot of what was wrong with her was shock. She was upset about her father, and she was angry at Jordan's arrogant attitude.

But she should never have made that last remark. It had been downright insulting. She opened up her mouth to apologise but the words just wouldn't come out.

Silence stretched and deepened and she felt even more uncomfortable.

She looked over at Jordan. His features seemed closed and very formidable in the half-light of the car. She wondered what he was thinking.

Probably that he wouldn't take a gold clock and sleep with her again either. At least he was gentlemanly enough not to say it.

She looked away from him again. They were in her road now and he was slowing down as they came to her apartment block. Charlotte searched for something to say, something that would lighten things between them again. After all, she had to face him at work tomorrow.

'Look, Jordan, you can't blame me for being upset. You have cast terrible aspersions on my father's character tonight—'

'I believe I said more about Ruth than your father,' Jordan cut across her calmly. 'I know you are angry, and worried about things. But just for the record I am not the villain of this piece. I'm the victim,' he said quietly.

She glanced over at him with a frown. Try as she did it was very hard to see Jordan Lynch in the role of victim: he was too self-assured, too arrogantly cool. And he did stand to come out of the whole sorry mess smelling of roses. He wanted control of her father's company and he was probably going to get what he wanted.

She looked away from him again back at her hands. That didn't mean what her father or Ruth had done—if indeed they had done anything, she reminded herself fiercely—was right.

'I realise I was probably out of order with the remarks I made about you being a charlatan,' she conceded in a low tone.

'Not probably, you *were* out of order.'

'Sorry.' She muttered the word almost under her breath.

'What did you say?'

'I think you heard me.' She glanced over at him sharply. 'I'm sorry, OK?'

'You don't like admitting that you're wrong, do you?' he said with sudden amusement.

She took a deep breath. 'Look, this might all be very amusing to you—'

'I can assure you I'm not that amused,' he cut across her heavily. 'Not with the position my company is in.'

'Oh, so it's *your* company already, is it?'

He pulled the car to a standstill. 'We will have to wait and see about that.'

'Yes, we'll have to wait and see.' Trying to make a dignified exit, she reached for the door handle. 'Thank you for the lift home,' she said with stiff politeness.

She got out of the car and headed for the front door, thinking he'd just drive away. But disconcertingly he turned off the engine and also got out of the car, following her towards her front door.

'We shouldn't argue,' he said gently. 'It's not going to solve anything.'

He watched the way her hand shook as she tried to put the key into her front door and then reached to take it from her. The touch of his hand against hers made her shiver deep inside. But it wasn't with anger—this was an emotion totally at the other end of the scale. She stepped away from him sharply. How could she feel passion for him after the words that had just passed between them?

Not only had he made love to her the other night and then bragged about it to someone at the other end of a phone, but he was also ruthlessly going to pursue her father for his shares. This was not a man to fantasise over.

If Jordan noticed how quickly she moved away from his touch, he said nothing. He simply pushed open the door and stood back to allow her to enter first.

He glanced around the apartment as he stepped inside, noting the beauty of the décor. Unlike his flat, which had a minimalist style, this was warm and feminine; there was a clever use of colour and lots of books and flowers.

'My father isn't hiding here,' she told him. 'If that's why you've come inside with me.'

'I never for one moment thought that he was.' Jordan took his coat off and threw it over a chair. 'After Ruth phoned me I checked and found the call was international.'

'I'll just call you Inspector Clouseau, shall I?' She couldn't help the sarcastic remark.

'If it makes you feel better, call me anything you like.' His voice was equally sardonic.

She watched as he walked into the lounge. 'Nice flowers,' he commented as his eyes lit on the crystal vase of red roses.

They had arrived from David the day before; absurdly, her first thought had been that Jordan had sent them…now, how crazy was that? Not quite as crazy as the pang of disappointment when she had discovered they were from David.

OK, David had cheated on her, but he suddenly seemed like a pretty safe alternative to the man roaming around her apartment.

'Are you going to make a coffee?' Jordan asked her

suddenly. 'Or are you going to just hover there looking nervous all night?'

'I'm not nervous!'

'Good.' He smiled at her. It was a particularly warm smile and it made little flutters of apprehension turn in her stomach. 'Black, no sugar.'

She turned away and went through to the kitchen. 'Man's a damn nightmare,' she muttered to herself.

'You know, talking to yourself is the first sign of madness,' Jordan called through from the other room.

She banged the coffee jar down from a cupboard. He could have instant and like it, she thought. Why had he come inside with her anyway?

She suddenly remembered the other night and how he'd been the one in the kitchen making coffee and she had been wandering around his lounge. More memories followed...how he'd kissed her and the heat of their passion had totally blown her away.

She remembered how she hadn't been able to get enough of him, how she had welcomed the feeling of his hands slipping beneath her blouse, unfastening her bra, finding the warmth of her skin and teasing and caressing her into complete arousal.

Her hand slipped as she picked up a china cup and it smashed on the floor.

'Need some help?'

Jordan's voice close behind her in the small confines of her kitchen made her nerves scream. 'No! I can manage, thank you.'

She bent down to pick the pieces up and promptly cut her wrist on a jagged edge. It was surprisingly deep and blood oozed from the gash.

Jordan was beside her in an instant. 'You need to bathe that,' he said, turning to run the tap on the kitchen sink.

She didn't protest as he put her hand under the running water.

'Have you got some antiseptic and a plaster?'

'Yes, there's a first-aid kit in the top cupboard.' She nodded towards the place she meant, and watched as he went straight to the box.

'I'll manage now, thanks,' she said as he took out the antiseptic and cotton wool.

'Don't be silly, it's your right hand. I'll do it for you.' Without waiting for her approval, he soaked the cotton wool in the antiseptic and then, taking her hand, dabbed it gently across the wound. It stung, and she winced and tried to pull away from him.

'Hold still,' he rebuked. 'It's a deep cut and it needs cleaning.'

Gently and thoroughly he rinsed the wound again before applying more antiseptic.

The stinging was fading but what was really bothering her now was this close contact. The touch of his hand against her skin was too familiar; it was making her feel hot and awkward.

'I'll take over now.' She tried to pull away from him but he wouldn't let her.

'Don't be such a baby. Just hold still,' he said firmly.

Charlotte glared at the top of his dark hair. This was pure, unmitigated torture. She felt clumsy and stupid…no, more than that, completely idiotic, because the way he was holding her wrist now made her remember how he had kissed it the other night, sending a flame of fire shooting straight through her heart.

She was fidgeting from foot to foot now, willing him to release her. It seemed an eternity before he finally stuck a plaster over the wound.

'You are such a baby.' He smiled up at her, his dark hazel eyes warmly teasing. She remembered how he had called her 'baby' when they were making love, but then it had been a husky endearment whispered close against her ear, as he took full possession of her body.

The memory made her feel as though someone had scalded her, and as he loosened his hold she wrenched away from him.

'Thanks,' she muttered. Self-consciously, she couldn't look him in the eye, but pretended to be examining the plaster.

'You're welcome.' His voice was sardonic. 'I wasn't going to eat you for supper, you know. There's no need to be so nervous.'

'I'm not nervous!' It was the second time she had said that to him tonight, and it was a downright lie. 'I'll make you that coffee.' She turned away from him and got another cup down from the cupboard.

Behind her she was aware of Jordan clearing up the broken crockery. She wanted to tell him to leave it, the kitchen was too small for them to be in together, but then so was the lounge—so was the whole damn apartment. If he were at the other end of a football pitch it would be too close for comfort.

As she turned to get milk from the fridge she almost walked into him. Awkwardly she sidestepped him. She'd never felt so acutely conscious of a man before. It was as if she had suddenly regressed to being a very young teenager again, hormones racing out of all control.

As she turned back to the coffee she found him barring her way. 'Are we going to call a truce, Charlotte?'

'A truce?' She looked up at him uncertainly.

'Well, we can't go on like this, can we?'

'I don't know what you mean.'

'I think you do.' He took the milk from her and put it down on the counter behind him.

'I'm sorry about what's happened, OK?'

Which particular thing was he sorry about? she wondered. Notching her up on his bedpost or accusing her stepmother of fraud?

She tried to step past him but he wouldn't let her. He put one hand behind her, resting on the fridge, so that she felt hemmed in.

She looked up into his eyes. It wasn't that he was too big for this kitchen: he was too big for her life.

'So are we going to work together to sort out this problem with your father?'

'I already told you I'd help you.'

'So why did you object so much to my questioning Jen?'

'There was no point to it and I was upset.'

'So are we on the same side in this business with your father, Charlie? I need to know.' He took hold of her chin, forcing her to look at him.

The touch of his hand made her tremble inside. She flinched away from him.

'Sorry.' He dropped his hand. 'I forgot that you don't like me to touch you.' The humour had a dry edge to it.

She looked up and met his eyes and tried to concentrate on her father, not that last remark. 'I find it hard to believe that Dad or Ruth would have taken that money. But if they have…I definitely don't think it's right.' She hesitated and her voice lowered. 'But he's still my father, Jordan. No matter what he's done, I still love him.' Her eyes pleaded with him to understand. 'So I can't be on your side. Unless…'

'Unless what?'

'You allow him some extra time to pay back the money that's missing.'

He dropped his hands.

'Please, Jordan.' Her voice was soft.

He looked deep into her green eyes; they looked wide and innocent, gently vulnerable. With a sigh he raked a hand through the darkness of his hair. 'All right…just for you.' The words lingered softly between them. 'But only an extra few days, OK? Don't be thinking I'm a pushover because I'm not.'

'OK.' She smiled at him. There was no way she would ever think Jordan Lynch was a pushover.

It was the first real smile she had given him all evening, Jordan thought. And it had probably just cost him dearly, because he did want control of the business and it needed to be sorted out sooner rather than later.

His eyes lingered for a moment on the softness of her lips, then moved down over the V-neck jumper she was wearing, its silky lines clinging to her curves. He wanted to take her into his arms, make love to her again; the need burnt inside and he could feel his body gearing up for it.

The phone in the lounge rang and it seemed to release them both from the sudden trance that had held them.

'I…I'd better get that.'

After quite a few bleeps, the answering machine cut in. 'Hi, Charlie, it's David again.'

The deep voice drifted clearly through to them. 'I hope you liked the flowers.'

Charlotte started to move hurriedly through to the lounge to pick up the receiver so that Jordan couldn't listen to this.

'Please forgive me and have dinner with me. We need to talk.'

He'd hung up before she got to the phone.

'Didn't give you much chance to answer, did he?' Jordan said drily from behind her.

'He probably didn't expect me to be in.'

'Maybe he's just a wimp and it's easier talking to the machine.' Jordan gave her a wry look. 'He sounded very contrite. What is he apologising for?'

'I don't want to talk about David if you don't mind.'

She moved past him back into the kitchen and brought their coffees through. When she returned he was looking at the answering machine. 'You've got six messages on here.'

'Have I?' She handed him his coffee.

'Maybe you should listen to them. There might be one from your father.'

'I'll listen to them later.'

'Why?'

'Because there might be something personal on there.'

'You can fast-forward the personal stuff.'

He was looking at her with the light of challenge in his eyes. 'I'm only interested in where your father is so we can talk to him. I thought we had an agreement, Charlie.'

She glared at him and then with a sigh pushed the play button on the machine.

'Hi, darling, it's me—' She snapped David's voice off very quickly. The tape wound on to the next call.

'It was a one-night stand! I love you—' David again. She snapped the tape off, feeling herself going red with embarrassment. The third one couldn't be David again, surely? Gingerly she pressed the play button once more.

'I know when we talked about marriage once…' She was in such a frantic scrabble to turn that particular piece of conversation off that she missed the button and it played too long. 'We could still make a go of things; I've had a change of—' The machine snapped off.

'That was just getting interesting,' Jordan said wryly. 'What do you think he's had a change of? Underpants?'

Charlotte glared at him. 'My telephone conversations are none of your business and I'm not playing this game any more.'

'You've only got a few more to go, and we know the last one is David again. They can't all be him. Surely he's fed up talking to a machine by now?'

Charlotte wasn't too sure. Her hand hovered over the machine. This was like playing Russian roulette.

Taking a deep breath, she pressed 'play' again. This time it was Ruth's voice that filled the room. 'Charlie, are you there?' There was a pause while she waited to see if the phone would be lifted. 'Charlie, I'm in desperate trouble...' Her voice cracked slightly as she continued. 'I borrowed some money from the business account. It's not what it seems but I'll explain that later. It was only supposed to be a temporary measure but things have gone horribly wrong and I don't know what to do. Can you come over here immediately because I really need your help? Take the address down. I'm in Port Grimaud...' Charlotte sprang up to scribble the address on the pad next to the phone. 'See you soon, I hope.' The phone went dead.

Tears sprang to Charlotte's eyes. So it was Ruth! Even now she couldn't believe it. She was so upset that she didn't turn the machine off and it went on to play the next message. It was David again. 'Charlotte, ring me immediately.'

Charlotte switched him off in full flow. She had more to worry about than David.

'That guy is a prat,' Jordan said in disgust.

Charlotte made no reply. She kept her head down so that Jordan couldn't see the tears in her eyes.

'Are you OK?' he asked softly.

She nodded, but still didn't look up. 'I just hated hearing Ruth so upset. Whatever possessed her to do it?'

Jordan made no reply. Then, all of a sudden, he put his coffee down on the table and reached for the phone.

'What are you doing?' Her head jerked up, her eyes wide. 'Jordan, what are you doing?'

Her heart started to thump in fear as he began to dial. 'You're not phoning the police, are you? I thought we had a deal! Please, Jordan! Don't!' She reached out to him, catching hold of his arm. 'I'll do anything...but please don't get the police.'

His eyes locked with hers. 'Anything?'

Her eyes were wide with anguish.

'Anything?' He shook his head and for a second his eyes moved over the sweetness of her curves. 'Let's see...' He reached out and touched the side of her face in a butterfly-soft caress. And despite everything she felt desire stir quite forcefully to life inside her.

'Pity I'm not really your type though. What was it you said—you'd rather make love with the devil than make love with me again?' he said laconically.

She felt her face flare with colour.

Then he pulled away from her as whoever was at the other end of the line answered. 'Hi, yes, I'm ringing to see when I can get two seats on the first available flight to Nice.'

Charlotte felt her skin colour change dramatically as the full horror of her mistake dawned on her. He hadn't been ringing the police at all.

'Tomorrow afternoon is fine,' Jordan continued calmly.

Why hadn't he just answered her when she'd questioned him? She wanted to curl up and die of embarrassment. She had thought that waking up in his bed had been mortifying but this...this was almost worse.

Jordan watched her as he spoke, noted the scalded colour of her cheeks.

'Yes, Jordan Lynch, Charlotte McCann.' He reached into his back pocket and brought out a wallet to find his credit card.

'Yes, OK, thanks.' The phone went down again. And there was the most awkward silence Charlotte had ever lived through.

'I thought you were ringing the police,' she said numbly.

'So I gathered.' His lips twisted in dry humour. 'I almost wish I had been now. That was a very interesting offer—tempting too.' His eyes flicked down over her body again and she felt them as if they were physically touching her. 'Trouble is, I like my women a little more willing. It would take the edge off things, knowing it was just payment in kind…so to speak.'

She averted her eyes from him awkwardly. 'Very funny, Jordan,' she said angrily. 'And when I said anything…I didn't mean *that.*'

'Really? Sounded like you meant *that* to me. Perhaps I could take a rain check and think about the idea,' he murmured, coming closer towards her.

He reached out, tipping her chin up and forcing her to look at him again. 'And for now I'll just take a kiss on account,' he said huskily.

She didn't say anything, just continued to stare up at him, her heart thumping so heavily against her chest she was sure he could hear it.

Jordan lowered his head and his mouth found hers. The kiss was gently persuasive and it made her insides turn to fire. His thumb stroked along the side of her jaw, holding her face up towards his, but he had no need to hold her still. When the kiss deepened she kissed him back hungrily, meeting the pressure of his lips with a desire that was raw with need. In those few minutes she forgot everything apart from the thrill of being in his arms.

He pulled back from her, his eyes raking over her upturned face, noting the softness of her lips, the dazed expression in her misty eyes.

'Not bad for a woman who said she didn't want me to touch her again,' he murmured. 'Can we leave my credit account open…because I'm going to have to leave now?'

She didn't answer him. Maybe this was funny to him, but she couldn't laugh. Her emotions were all over the place.

He turned away from her and picked up his coat from the chair. 'You had better throw a few things into a bag for tomorrow. We'll leave for the airport straight from the office. That way at least we'll get a chance to organise things at work before we go.'

How could he talk so coolly about work after the emotions that had just ricocheted through them? Charlotte wondered fiercely. But she already knew the answer: he could switch his mind to work because he hadn't felt the same depth of desire. Lovemaking was just a game to him. All Jordan really cared about was getting her father's business.

The front door closed quietly behind him and she pressed her hand against her lips. They felt as if they were still throbbing and her body was alive with an aching need for him to come back and finish what he'd started. It was mortifying that a man who felt so little for her could turn her on so much.

CHAPTER FIVE

'HOW come you're suddenly rushing off to the south of France?' Frank looked at the overnight case that was sitting by her office door.

'There's some land ripe for development that Jordan wants to look at.' The lie tripped off her tongue: this was the second time she had issued it this morning and it was getting easier. 'Also, there are some documents I need Dad to look at.'

Jennifer had laughed when she had told her this. 'I've heard everything now, sis,' she had said. 'But you can't kid me. You're off on a romantic few days to the sun.'

Charlotte had pretended to laugh as well, glad that her sister had no inkling of what was going on.

Her assistant, Frank, wasn't laughing though. He just looked concerned. 'The business isn't going under, is it?' he asked abruptly.

'Going under?' Charlotte stopped what she was doing and looked up at him. 'No! Whatever makes you think that?'

Frank Simmons, a good-looking man in his late twenties, shrugged and looked slightly uncomfortable. 'There have been rumours flying around because of your father failing to come back to work.'

'Have there?' Charlotte was genuinely surprised. She hadn't heard any rumours, but then she spent the majority of her time either buried in here under a weight of paper or downstairs in the workshop.

'Well, tell everyone that the business is perfectly OK.

Dad is just taking a well-earned rest. He deserves it, you know.'

Frank nodded and put some papers down on her desk. 'You had better take these with you. It's the spec for the new apartments over in Richmond; there's an artist's impression of the building and the measurements for the interior. You need to get in contact with the suppliers as well—I said you'd phone tomorrow because—'

'Yes, OK. I'll take all this with me and phone them from my mobile.'

So much for Jen's impression that she was going to have a few days' rest, she thought as she put the paperwork on the growing pile beside her ready to go into her briefcase. She was taking enough work to last a week: hopefully they would return tomorrow, but there was no knowing for sure when they would be back.

Charlotte glanced across towards Jordan's office. She had dreaded facing him this morning but they had both been so busy that it had been all right. There had been a few moments first thing when he had come into her office and her blood pressure had risen dramatically but he had been completely laid-back, as if the phone call from Ruth had never taken place—or the kiss that followed.

'The official line is that we are going to France to look at some land and to get your father to sign some papers, OK?' he had said easily as he put some memos down on her desk.

'Fine.'

He had turned to leave the office almost immediately and she had been the one to detain him. 'Jordan, should I get Frank to sort us out a hotel?'

'No need,' he had said, closing the door behind him.

Why wouldn't he let her get a hotel? she wondered now. They were definitely going to need one. By her reckoning the flight would land in Nice about five-thirty local time, and it was another few hours down to Port Grimaud. As they had no return flight booked, it surely would be tomorrow at the earliest before they were able to come back.

Suddenly she remembered something Jordan had said to Jen about owning a piece of property over there. Was he thinking that they could stay there? Charlotte wasn't so sure she liked the thought of that. A hotel would be better, less intimate than them being alone together in some apartment.

'I'll be back as soon as possible,' she told Frank, dragging her attention from Jordan. 'Will you be able to deal with things in here?'

'Of course,' Frank said easily. 'Oh, and by the way, Ruth was on the phone earlier. You were on the other line so I asked if she could leave a message or phone back.'

'What did she say?' Charlotte asked, instantly alert.

'She said she'd phone back.'

Charlotte stared at him in complete frustration. 'Did she at least leave a new number that I could contact her on?'

Frank shook his head.

'Well, if she rings again, I want you to give her priority. Put her straight through to me.'

'Fine! Don't worry,' he drawled with a grin.

'No, I mean it, Frank. It's important.' She stared at him earnestly.

'I'll put her straight through.' He held up his hands. 'Promise.'

'Thanks.' She took a deep breath.

'You need a break, Charlie,' he said, shaking his head as he went out of the door. 'You're working too hard.'

A good night's sleep would do, Charlotte thought grimly. She had hardly slept a wink last night, her mind had been so filled with worries about Ruth and her father, and disturbing thoughts of Jordan.

The strange thing was that the one person who had been

missing from her thoughts recently was David—the person that, up to a few short weeks ago, she had thought she was going to spend the rest of her life with. Life could be very unexpected sometimes.

As the plane levelled out Charlotte started to relax. She hated take-offs: in fact her heart had been pumping in her chest almost as hard as when Jordan had kissed her. Immediately the thought crossed her mind she wished it hadn't. She was trying to forget Jordan's kisses.

Charlotte glanced sideways at him. He was reading a business report, had been immersed in it from the moment they had got into the taxi outside the office until now. Her eyes moved over the lightweight grey suit he was wearing—it was very classy, and looked just right teamed with his silver-blue shirt. In fact, he looked altogether too attractive for her peace of mind.

The air stewardess obviously thought so too. She smiled very provocatively at Jordan as she came down the aisle with the drinks trolley.

'Drinks from the bar, sir?'

Jordan looked over at Charlotte and she weakened to a glass of wine. Jordan just had a cola.

'Do you ever drink alcohol?' she asked him before he returned his attention to his report.

'Occasionally, but never when I drive.'

Now she came to think about it, she had hardly ever seen him with a glass of alcohol in his hand. Even when they'd had dinner together he'd had a soft drink.

The pilot interrupted their conversation to tell them what altitude they were flying at and that the weather in Nice was a favourable twenty-eight degrees.

'Not a bad temperature for this time of the year,' Jordan remarked.

'Better than London, that's for sure.' Suddenly Charlotte

found herself wishing that Jen had been right in her assumptions and that this was just a romantic pleasure trip, just her and Jordan and nothing else to worry about. The thought seemed like heaven.

She was obviously going mad, she thought sardonically. Maybe Frank was right and she was more in need of a holiday than she'd thought. Having a romantic liaison with Jordan would be asking for trouble. And she was still fretting about the way he had wound her up with that telephone call last night.

She glanced over at him again. Trouble was, it was hard to stay cross with him for very long. He was giving her father more time and he was reasonable enough to want to come out here and speak to him face to face. He didn't have to do that. Especially as they were so busy in the office.

Was he going to spend the whole flight with his head in that report? she wondered. She should be pleased—at least when he was working he wasn't teasing her unmercifully, something he seemed exceptionally good at. How was it that Jordan Lynch was such an enigma to her? She felt she couldn't really get a handle on knowing him. OK, they had slept together, but she still didn't really know him, not properly. The fact made her uncomfortable.

She had known David for ages before she had slept with him. They had met at a business fair on interior design and had struck up a friendship. But it was only within the last two years that their relationship had become intimate. At one time, if someone had asked her to sum David up in three words she would have said solid, dependable and level-headed. But if he had been any of those things he wouldn't have jumped into bed with one of her best friends. She switched her mind abruptly away from that.

'So why didn't you let me ask Frank to book us into a hotel for tonight?' she asked Jordan.

'Because we may as well stay at my place; it's just across the bay from Port Grimaud.' He hardly glanced up from his paperwork.

'Wouldn't a hotel be better?'

'Why?'

She had his attention now.

'Well, for one thing it would be less trouble for one night. No making up beds.' Deliberately she used the plural. She didn't want him getting any wrong ideas after last night's little fiasco.

His eyes roved over her face. He looked amused for a second and she could feel herself growing warm. 'Don't worry; you won't have to make up any *beds*. I have an arrangement with a woman who comes in and sees to all of that for me.'

She watched him as he returned his attention to his papers.

There was a few minutes' silence between them. Charlotte fidgeted in her seat and looked out of the window. She told herself that she should get some of her own work done. But her mind wouldn't settle. She didn't want to work, she wanted to talk to Jordan. 'So how come you own a place over in France anyway?' she asked, finally giving in to her curiosity.

'My ex-wife is French. After the divorce Nadine got our house in Paris and I got the place in the south, which was our holiday home.'

'Did you argue about who was keeping what?' She didn't know why she asked that, or why she was so curious about his past life.

He put down his papers. 'No, we didn't argue at all. It was remarkably civil. And neither of us wanted the holiday home...in fact, I haven't been out here since the divorce just over a year ago.'

'A year is a long time to have a property and not use it.'

'I suppose it is.' He was reading his papers again and she had the distinct impression he really didn't want to talk about this any further.

But Charlotte wanted to ask him more. It was only the memory of that picture of his little girl that stopped her. She knew Jordan didn't like to talk about the past; maybe some things were just too painful to talk about, especially on a plane at thirty-two thousand feet when he was trying to concentrate on work.

'I'm really worried about Ruth,' she told him, switching the subject. 'She phoned me again this morning, at the office this time.'

'What did she say?' He looked over at her with a frown.

'I never got to speak to her. I was on the other line to the fabric warehouse at the time and Frank didn't realise it was important. She said she'd ring back. I tried Dad's mobile again but it's still switched off. Maybe it's just as well because if he had answered I wouldn't have known what to say.' She sighed. 'I wish Ruth had been more forthright with her explanations.'

'Well, we'll find out soon enough what it's all about.'

'Yes.' The words made her apprehension about the situation increase. She took a sip of her wine and looked out of the window at the clear blue sky.

Charlotte wondered how this whole sorry mess was going to affect her father's marriage. She hated to think of him being in such a vulnerable position; he'd always been so strong, so kind and wise. Well, she was just going to have to be there for him now and help him through whatever mess needed to be cleared up.

She remembered suddenly how he had drawn her to one side, before he had made Jennifer the wedding gift of her house. 'I want you to know, Charlie that the business will be yours one day,' he had said gently. 'Just in case you are thinking that these gifts are a bit one-sided.'

She had told him she didn't want or expect anything from him, that she was quite happy with the way things were.

'Yes, but my hopes for the future of the business rest with you,' he had said solemnly.

The words rang in her head.

She had really meant it when she had told her father she didn't expect anything from him. And she still didn't; she was well able to stand on her own.

'I hope this won't be the end of Dad and Ruth's marriage.' She blurted out her fears, unable to keep them to herself a moment longer.

'I hope not.' Jordan paused before asking cautiously, 'How did you feel about your father marrying Ruth?'

She looked at him with some surprise. 'I was delighted. Both Jennifer and I felt so happy for him. He deserved to find happiness after all he'd been through. And he had been on his own for so long.'

His eyes were gentle on her face. 'What happened to your mother?' he asked.

'She died of cancer when I was sixteen.'

She looked away from him out of the window so that he couldn't see the emotion in her eyes.

Jordan's hand covered hers on the seat rest between them; the warm touch made her heart miss a beat.

'Do you know there is a rumour going around the office that we are in trouble and might be folding?' She tried to change the subject.

'Yes, I heard. I've just been waiting to sort things out with your father before I scotch it,' he said gently. 'It's because he's stayed away for so long. People aren't stupid; they know Simon lives, eats and breathes the company. So they know something is up.'

The seatbelt sign came on and the pilot told them they were about to make their final descent into Nice Airport. Jordan released her hand to pack up his papers and fold away the tables in front of them.

'Don't worry any more, Charlotte,' he said. 'We'll sort things out together.'

Charlotte could feel her stomach dipping as the altitude dropped…or was that simply caused by the gentle way Jordan had spoken?

It was hot as they walked out of the terminal and Charlotte wished she'd had time to change out of her black business suit before travelling. It felt very inappropriate for this climate. She took off her jacket and pushed up the sleeves of her white blouse as she stood waiting for Jordan, who was talking to the car-hire people. Then she searched in her handbag and found a tie for her hair so that she could pull it up off the back of her neck.

'Feeling the heat?' Jordan asked with a grin as he strolled back over to her and noted the change of hairstyle and attire.

'I should have worn something cooler. It's hard to believe it can be so much warmer after such a short flight,' she said.

'You'll feel better when we get in the car and I turn on the air-conditioning.' He picked up her bag and her briefcase.

'It's OK, I can manage those,' she said. But he was already striding ahead with them.

They located their hire car and Jordan threw everything into the boot. 'What on earth have you got in that briefcase?' he asked with amusement as they turned to get into the vehicle. 'It's almost heavier than your overnight bag.'

'My workload for tomorrow. I suppose I should have

been like you and done some of it on the plane, but somehow I couldn't settle to concentrate.'

'You must be worried,' Jordan murmured sardonically. 'One thing I've noticed about you over this last year is that you always seem to put work first.'

'Do I?' She glanced over at him as he started the car engine. Somehow it bothered her that this was what stood out about her. 'Are you trying to tell me that I'm boringly sensible?'

'Are you fishing for compliments?' he countered, grinning teasingly at her.

'No.' She felt her skin burn and was glad when the air-conditioning came on and the vents blasted her with cool air. 'I was just curious as to how you perceive me.'

'I think I could be in a lot of hot water if I answer that,' he said with a definite glint of humour in his voice.

Now, what did he mean by that? 'Well, I hope you're not judging me on last night,' she ventured, feeling her pulses start to race. 'Because I wasn't offering you my body, you know. You just jumped to the wrong conclusion.'

'Did I?' Jordan smiled. 'Why would I have done that?'

'Because you've got a one-track mind, of course.'

Jordan laughed, but didn't say anything. He was busy manoeuvring his way through the traffic.

They travelled in silence for a while. Jordan seemed to know the roads well, and he was a good driver, she noticed. His reactions were fast and he handled the powerful car well.

Surreptitiously she watched his face. He looked so very much in control of everything around him. It made her feel very safe and protected. David had never made her feel like this.

'Thanks for doing this, Jordan,' she said suddenly.

'Doing what?' He glanced at her.

'Taking the time out from the office to sort this matter out with Dad. And giving him more time...you know...' She shrugged.

'You've already thanked me for that.' He grinned. 'One kiss on account, wasn't that how it went?'

'Something like that.' She tried to make light of the subject the way he did, but she could feel her senses clamouring as she remembered that kiss. Maybe she needed to put him straight on a few things, she thought suddenly. Maybe she needed to be truthful and tell him she didn't view sex in the same casual way he did. Then maybe he would stop winding her up about it.

They lapsed into silence. They were on the motorway now, sailing along at top speed.

She looked over at him again and took a deep breath. 'Jordan, I want to tell you something.' She cleared her throat nervously.

'This sounds serious.' He glanced at her.

'You know the other night when we...made love...?'

'Yes.'

'Well, I've never done anything like that before.'

'David is even more stupid than I first thought, then,' Jordan murmured drily.

'I don't mean I haven't been to bed with a man before!' She glared at him. 'I mean I've never had a one-night stand before.'

'If this is your ham-fisted way of telling me that you were on the rebound from David the other night, I wouldn't bother, Charlotte,' he said acerbically. 'I think I've already figured that out for myself.'

She frowned and opened her mouth to tell him she wasn't on the rebound from David, that in the last few days she'd hardly given David a second thought. Then she closed her mouth again. Maybe being on the rebound was as good an excuse as any for that night of madness.

She looked away from him and thought that she probably shouldn't have said anything, but something perversely made her carry on. 'Anyway,' she muttered, 'I just thought I'd tell you because really I'm quite old-fashioned when it comes to affairs of the heart.'

'Nothing wrong with that,' Jordan said lightly.

'Any minute now you are going to tell me in a very patronising tone that you believed in love once upon a time as well.'

'Yes, I did.' He glanced over and their eyes locked for a second before he looked back at the road in front. 'Once upon a time.'

Charlotte supposed he was talking about his ex-wife. She wondered what Nadine had been like. Probably extremely stylish; all French women were stylish. If she closed her eyes she could almost picture her: petite, with dark hair, ultra-feminine.

'But now you like to love them and leave them and concentrate on your business ventures?' she said lightly.

'Is that how you perceive me?'

'You do have a lot of glamorous women in your life.'

'Not all at once though,' he laughed. 'You make me sound like a woman-eating monster.'

'I don't think you're a monster,' she said quickly. 'In fact, in a lot of ways you seem to be a pretty decent bloke.'

'Well, thanks…' He slanted a wry glance over at her. 'I think.'

She looked away from him. She hadn't told him that when she relaxed and allowed him to be in control it made her feel safe, or that her insides turned to liquid jelly when he smiled at her in a certain way. Or that she liked the way he kissed her. Or that he made her laugh…or that he was very, very good in bed. He was big-headed enough. Besides, she didn't want him bragging about her on the phone again!

They travelled on in silence. Charlotte noticed how quickly the daylight faded into night. The powerful gleam of headlights on the road ahead was almost mesmerising and she felt sleepy for a while.

But as the road signs for Port Grimaud came into sight she was instantly wide awake. 'Are we going straight to find Dad?' she asked, her attention moving to what lay ahead.

'Yes, I think it's best we get things sorted out as quickly as possible, don't you?'

'Yes, of course,' she agreed with him and felt the prickle of anxiety and unease about this situation return in full force.

The determination in his tone reminded her clearly that behind the charming façade that Jordan was able to project when it suited him, his first priority was the business.

They drove from the main road down towards huge gates that were manned by security guards.

'What kind of place is this?' Charlotte said in surprise.

'The kind of place where millionaires and movie stars hang out.' Jordan smiled. 'Sit tight for a moment, while I go and talk to the guard, tell him who we are here to see and reassure him that we are not members of the paparazzi out to cause trouble.'

Charlotte watched as he got out of the car and walked over to the security guard. He was back within a few minutes and they drove on past the guards and into the tree-lined streets beyond.

It was too dark to clearly see the village they had entered. But Charlotte had the impression of a yachting community: there were waterways and inlets at every turn and by the light of the street lamps it had a mystical stillness.

'This is the address,' Jordan said, slowing the car.

'Are you sure?' Charlotte followed his gaze up towards

a large private house that was in complete darkness. 'I thought they would be in a hotel.'

'This is the address that Ruth left on your machine.' Jordan switched off the car engine. 'Stay here and I'll investigate.'

Charlotte wasn't about to be left behind. This was her father and she wanted to be there to help in any way she could when Jordan confronted him.

'I thought I told you to stay in the car,' Jordan muttered with irritation as she caught up with him by the front gate.

'You are not my keeper, Jordan,' she said, moving swiftly ahead of him to walk down the path towards the front door. There was no bell so Charlotte rapped several times with the wrought-iron knocker. The sound vibrated on the wooden door and they stood and listened for any movement within.

There was silence except for the whistling of the rigging on nearby yachts as the breeze playfully caught them.

'There doesn't seem to be anyone in,' Charlotte murmured, reaching to knock again. Impatiently Jordan moved away from her, following the path around the side of the house.

'Where are you going?' she called after him.

'Doing a little investigating of my own,' he said without breaking his stride.

'Jordan!' Nervously she hurried after him. 'You can't go snooping around like this.'

'Watch me,' he said grimly. As if to prove the point he climbed agilely over a wrought-iron gate that barred his way.

'Jordan.' she called after him but he didn't turn back and, after a few moments' hesitation, Charlotte kicked off her high heels and followed him. It wasn't hard to get over the gate because it wasn't too high, but she had to leave her shoes behind. It was pitch black around the side of the house, forcing her to slow her steps and proceed cautiously in her bare feet. The scent of jasmine and bougainvillea mingled with the salt of the sea and as she turned the corner she could see the Mediterranean bathed in the soft glow of moonlight, and realised that what she had thought was the front of the house was in fact the back. The house faced out over the bay, the waters of the Med lapping directly in front of it. A huge white cabin cruiser was moored alongside a private jetty and there was an enormous patio area with wooden decking and a barbecue area.

'Well, they're definitely out.' Jordan distracted her attention from the beauty of their surroundings as he strolled over to stand by her side. 'There is no car in the garage.'

'Obviously they're out,' Charlotte murmured. 'We hardly needed to come skulking around here to discover that. If they had been in, they would have answered the door.'

'Not necessarily.' Jordan walked onto the patio and peered through the sliding glass doors into the darkened rooms beyond.

Charlotte glared at him. He was really starting to annoy her now. 'My father wouldn't hide from me, Jordan, if that's what you're trying to insinuate.'

'I'm not trying to insinuate anything.' Jordan moved to look through one of the other windows. 'I'm just checking all the possibilities.'

His calm, matter-of-fact manner didn't do anything to improve Charlotte's mood. 'Perhaps I should start raking through the undergrowth at the side of the house?' she suggested sarcastically. 'Just in case they are hiding under a gooseberry bush?'

He glanced over at her then and grinned. 'By all means. Don't let me detain you from the task.'

'This isn't funny, Jordan,' she said angrily.

'You're the one cracking the jokes.'

'You're the one dragging my father's reputation through the mud.' She put one hand on her hip.

'Not without provocation.'

'My father wouldn't hide from me. If he was here, he'd open the door.' For a second her voice trembled precariously, revealing the extent of her anxiety, and then she swung away to go and stand at the end of the patio, staring out across the sea at the lights that glittered on the other side of the bay, trying desperately to pull herself together.

'Well, you're right about one thing. There's no one in.' Jordan came to stand behind her and she noticed how his voice had softened. 'I suggest we go home and forget about this for tonight.'

Charlotte wished she could forget about it. But the worry about her father just seemed to be increasing inside her.

'Charlotte?' He put a gentle hand on her shoulder. 'Come on, I didn't mean to upset you. It's late and we're both tired.'

'This might not even be the right address.' She pulled away from the touch of his hand and turned to look at him. 'You could have made a mistake.'

'I haven't made a mistake,' Jordan said calmly.

'No, sorry, silly me. Jordan Lynch doesn't make mistakes, does he? Not like the rest of the human race.'

'Believe it or not, I have made my fair share of them,' Jordan replied impassively, taking hold of her arm. 'Now, come on, let's go home.'

'Home is hundreds of miles away, Jordan,' she muttered, trying to shrug off his hand as he started to propel her towards the side of the house. 'And I think I'd prefer just to wait here and see if Dad arrives.'

'Home for tonight is my place, which is a few more miles down the coast.' He didn't release her until they reached the side gate. 'And anyway, it's infinitely more sensible for us to face your father after a decent night's rest, when we are both thinking more clearly.'

The words dispelled the red heat of anger clouding her mind and brought a chilling clarity. He was right, she thought as she watched him climb over the gate. It would be in all their interests if Jordan was in a good frame of mind in the morning.

Suddenly it struck her forcibly all over again just how vulnerable they were. It was obvious Ruth had done something wrong, otherwise she would never have made that phone call. And if Jordan decided to prosecute they would be in a terrible mess. That the future happiness of her family could rest on something as flimsy as Jordan Lynch's goodwill was extremely sobering.

Jordan reached out a hand to help her as she started to climb over the gate to join him.

'I can manage, thank you,' she said.

'OK, Miss Independent,' Jordan murmured.

She bit back a sarcastic reply and then promptly lost her balance as one foot connected with firm ground and the other with a stray shoe. Jordan caught her as she stumbled and for a second she found herself in the warm circle of his arms.

It was the strangest sensation being so close to him. The familiar scent of his aftershave and the gentleness of his arms assailed her senses, stirring up a weakness and longing for him that was deeply disturbing, whilst at the same time strong, sensible voices inside were telling her in no uncertain terms that this man wanted control of the family business, that he was therefore her father's enemy and she must beware.

'Are you OK?' he asked softly.

'Yes, of course.' She pulled away from him sharply and busied herself finding her shoes and slipping them on. 'You're right, we should go back to your place and have an early night. We'll need a clear mind for tomorrow.'

CHAPTER SIX

'CHARLOTTE, we're here.'

As the car pulled to a standstill, her eyes flew open. 'Sorry,' she murmured sleepily. 'I closed my eyes for a moment and I shouldn't have done.'

'That's OK; it's been a long day.'

'I wasn't asleep, I was thinking about this situation with Dad. If that was the right address, I wonder—'

'Charlotte, you've worried enough about that today. Just leave it now,' he cut across her firmly.

'Easy for you to say,' she murmured. 'I can't just switch off—'

'I know.' Jordan cut across her again, but this time his voice was gentle. 'If it is any consolation, I do understand how you must be feeling.'

'Do you?'

His eyes moved over the pallor of her skin, the bright glitter of her eyes. 'Yes.' His voice was huskily soft. 'And I hate to see you so upset, Charlie.'

She couldn't find her voice to reply to that because suddenly from nowhere a lump had appeared in her throat. How was it that Jordan could be so damn irritating one moment and then so warm and understanding the next?

He switched off the car headlights, plunging them into complete darkness. She could just make out the shadowy outline of a large house against the night sky.

'Have you got an apartment here?' she asked as he reached for the door handle.

'No. It's just a house. Come on, let's get inside and I'll put some lights on so we can see what we're doing.'

The first thing that hit Charlotte as she stepped out of the car was the tropically strident sound of cicadas. Obviously Jordan's house was in the countryside. A warm breeze rustled through the palm trees—she could see their tall, dark silhouettes moving against the moonlit sky—and as her eyes became accustomed to the darkness it soon became apparent that this wasn't *just* a house, as Jordan had nonchalantly stated. It was a very beautiful villa with graceful lines that seemed straight out of a book on the best of French architecture—a high-pitched roof and square classical lines, enormous long windows covered by wooden shutters and elegant steps up to the front door.

She watched as Jordan found the keys and opened the door. 'You go on inside; I'll get the luggage,' he said as he switched on some lights.

Charlotte stepped inside. The hallway had black stone flags and white walls. It led through to an enormous lounge with large windows looking out towards the sea. As if in keeping with the nautical theme, the settees were blue against plain white walls. A large stone fireplace filled one wall and plain rugs covered a wooden floor that gleamed under the crystal lights like the deck of a ship.

Wandering over towards the windows, Charlotte looked down at the gardens. A pool was illuminated a brilliant turquoise against the darkness of the lawns.

'This is some place,' she murmured in admiration as Jordan came into the room behind her.

'Yes, it's OK.' He sounded coolly indifferent. 'Would you like something to eat and maybe a coffee?'

'I think just the coffee would be lovely; it's a bit late for eating. I'd like to take a shower first. Would you mind?' She looked around at him.

'No, of course not; go right ahead. I've put your bag in your room—it's the second on the right at the top of the stairs.'

As she moved past him she noticed he was looking at the room as if deep in thought—as if she wasn't even there.

She wondered what he was thinking about as she went out and up the stairs. Maybe the last time he had been here had been with his wife?

She walked along the corridor, noticing all the doors were closed except for that of the room Jordan had directed her to. It was as lovely as the rest of the house—plain white walls and an enormous double bed dressed in pure white linen. The only colour was the black wrought-iron bedstead and the pictures of tropical gardens on the walls. There was an *en suite* bathroom in the same cool white.

Charlotte lost no time stripping off and climbing into a warm shower. It was bliss to stand under the forceful jet of water, allowing the journey and the stresses of the day to wash away. She felt a hundred times better when she got out and wrapped herself in one of the white fluffy bath sheets. Wrapping her hair turban-style in another towel, she padded back through to the bedroom and opened her case.

Charlotte hadn't brought much in the way of clothes, just a dress, a pair of jeans and a few tops. She didn't relish the thought of putting on any of them. Her hand lingered over her blue silk nightdress and matching dressing gown. As it was after eleven o'clock, maybe it would be OK to put them on—she'd have a cup of coffee and turn in for the night.

Quickly she dressed in the nightwear and then gave her hair a blast with her hairdryer. She'd almost finished drying it when she heard Jordan's voice calling her. Tying the belt firmly around the waist on her dressing gown, she went downstairs to see what he wanted.

There was no one in the lounge. She wandered through to the kitchen, her eyes flicking over the modern eggshell-blue cupboards and beech counters. There was a very nice smell of food in here that, despite her earlier comments, made her feel quite hungry.

'There you are.' Jordan came in from the other door. 'I know you said you didn't want anything, but I've made us some supper.' His eyes took in the slender lines of her body in the blue silk.

'Oh! Sorry, I'd have got dressed if I'd known.' She felt suddenly awkward. 'I was just going to turn in.'

'You look fine the way you are,' he said. 'And you really should eat something, Charlotte.'

'Yes, I suppose you're right… Thanks, I will.'

He smiled.

'Would you like a glass of wine? There's a bottle in the fridge.'

'No, I'll just stick with coffee, thanks.' She went over to put the kettle on. Then leaned back against the counter as she waited for it to boil, watching Jordan as he moved around the kitchen. She noticed that he had changed into jeans and a T-shirt and that his hair was still damp from a shower. 'You're a fast worker. You've showered, changed and now you're making supper!'

'It's just an omelette.' He smiled. 'I thought it best to stick to something light at this time of night.'

She watched as he put a dressing on a salad and tossed it. He seemed quite at home in a kitchen, she thought. Watching him, it was almost hard to believe that he was the same high-powered businessman that she worked with, the same man who had told her with cold determination that he wanted complete control of the business. But he was and she needed to remember that at all times, she told herself as her thoughts started to veer towards how attractive he was.

She turned away from him to make the coffee. 'Jordan, how much money is actually missing from the company?'

She tried to make her voice light as she asked the question for the second time. 'You never told me the exact amount.'

The query met with silence and she looked back over at him.

'Let's not go there, Charlotte.' His dark eyes met hers steadily and very seriously. 'Let's just relax tonight, pretend the business doesn't exist.'

'I've never been one for burying my head in the sand,' she said with quiet dignity.

Jordan noticed how ramrod straight she held herself. She had given a lot towards the business and this couldn't be easy for her.

As he named the sum of money involved he watched the colour drain away from her skin. 'As I said to you in London, if your father can't afford to pay it back then we'll come to an agreement with regards to the shares of the business.'

Although Jordan's voice was nonchalant there was a steely undertone that she heard very clearly.

'And that's what you really want, the shares in the company.'

'You know it is.' His eyes narrowed on her face. 'This won't affect your job, Charlotte. I'll be relying on you more than ever to run the design department when I take over.'

She noticed how he spoke as if this was already a done deal and felt a spurt of anger. 'I think you mean *if* you take over,' she reminded him, then flashed him a bright smile to accompany the tough tone.

'You've got guts, Charlotte, I'll give you that,' he said quietly. 'I have a feeling that you would fight to your last breath to protect someone you love and believe in.'

'You're right, I would.' She met his eyes steadily. 'I just hope it won't come to that.'

'So do I.' He nodded. 'The last thing I want is to be on opposite sides from you.'

That was the last thing Charlotte wanted as well, and it wasn't just because she knew Jordan would make a formidable adversary. There was something that drew her to him, some weakness that stirred within her when he looked at her in a certain way; she couldn't exactly say what it was...and she wished it would go away because the situation she was trapped in was complicated enough.

'But getting back to what I was saying about your job. No matter what happens, I will want you to stay on.' His voice was firm.

'We'll have to wait and see how things go.' She kept her voice deliberately vague.

Jordan wasn't happy about that. In fact the idea of not having Charlotte around in the office was quite horrifying.

'Now, do you want any help with that omelette?' she asked brightly. 'Because I'm suddenly starving.'

He hesitated then allowed the subject of work to drop. There would be plenty of time to discuss the situation later. They both needed to relax now.

'No, you go and sit down. The table is laid outside. I won't be long.'

Charlotte picked up the coffee-pot and headed outside. She paused in the doorway as she saw the table out on the terrace. It was laid perfectly with a white tablecloth and candles. 'You seem to have gone to a lot of trouble,' she murmured, looking back at him.

'Well, I think after the day we've had we owe ourselves a little respite, don't you?'

Maybe he was right, she thought as she sat at the table and sipped her coffee. It had been a really long day and it was soothing sitting out here. The night was beautiful, not a cloud in the star-studded sky, and the air felt heavy and drowsy with the scent of flowers. The only sounds were those of the cicadas and the gentle whisper of the breeze. She put her cup down and stretched her hands upwards, rolling her head around to release the tension in her neck.

She stopped abruptly as she looked up and saw Jordan standing beside her at the table. 'Is this another one of your toning exercises?' he asked with a smile. 'Like crawling around on the floor first thing in the morning?'

She tried very hard not to lose her composure at the blatant reminder of their night together. She gave a small laugh. 'I was just unwinding that's all. Everything feels as if it needs stretching out.'

'Well, don't stop on my account.' Jordan put her meal in front of her and then sat down opposite. 'In fact, maybe you'd like a hand?' he asked, his eyes dipping to where her dressing gown had parted slightly and he could see the creamy curve of her skin.

'No, thank you.' She smiled at him. 'And if you're trying to embarrass me it won't work. I'm through getting hot and bothered around you.'

Jordan laughed at that. 'Now, that is a pity,' he drawled teasingly.

Carefully she ignored him and concentrated on the food instead. 'This is good,' she said, tucking into the omelette. 'Who did all the shopping for you?'

'Madeline. She's the woman I was telling you about on the plane.'

'Ah, yes, the woman you have the arrangement with.'

'She's a neighbour, a very good one as well. She organised a cleaner to come in for me and generally keeps an eye on everything. I don't know what I would have done without her over the last year.'

Charlotte glanced over at the pool shimmering in the artificial lights that lit it from beneath. 'How could you bear not to come here for so long?' she asked him suddenly. 'It's so beautiful.'

When he didn't answer straight away she looked over at him. The handsome features were serious now and there was no hint of the light-hearted man of a moment ago.

'Jordan?' she prompted him softly.

He shrugged. 'To be honest with you, I never wanted to come back here again. There are too many memories.'

'Of your ex-wife?'

'And of Natasha. Of the night we lost her.'

'It happened here?' Charlotte stared at him in consternation. No wonder he had looked strained when he walked into this house.

'It was a car crash while we were here on holiday.'

'I'm so sorry, Jordan.' Her voice was a mere whisper on the gentleness of the warm breeze. 'Maybe we should have booked into a hotel. It must be very painful for you coming back here.'

'I did think about a hotel. But what's the point when this place is sitting here?' He glanced back at the house. 'And anyway, I don't have to be here for the memories to pack their punches—that can happen anywhere.' He looked over at her. 'In the middle of a conversation or at work…or when I look at a child.' He shrugged. 'Even seeing Harriet. Natasha would have been about her age now.'

Charlotte desperately wanted to get up and go and put her arms around him. 'Losing a child must be the worst thing in the world,' she said softly. 'And to lose her in an accident…' She trailed off, words failing her. 'Were you driving?'

He shook his head. 'I was finishing up some paperwork that I had brought with me.' His words were resigned and flat. 'Nadine had taken Natasha down to the village to buy some milk. They were only supposed to be fifteen minutes. I often think, if only we'd done the shopping the night before, or if only I hadn't been doing that damn paper-work.'

'You can't blame yourself.' Charlotte frowned. 'Or your ex-wife. Accidents happen; life isn't always fair.'

Jordan's lips twisted wryly. 'I know that.'

Looking across at him, Charlotte wondered if it had been the strain of losing their child that had torn his marriage apart. Something like that would be hard to deal with.

'I wish there was something I could say to make you feel better,' she said quietly.

He smiled over at her. 'Just having you here when I walked through the front door helped,' he said.

She felt her heart miss several beats as she looked over into his eyes.

'I don't think I realised just how much I didn't want to face this place on my own until today.'

The shrill ring of the telephone coming from the house broke the mood, and Jordan pushed his chair away from the table. 'Won't be a minute,' he said.

Charlotte watched a moth fluttering too close to the flame of the candle as she waited for him to come back. She thought over the tragedy that had torn his life apart. He seemed so strong, so indomitable most of the time, the tough businessman who got his own way in most things. And yet beneath that tough surface there was another man, a different man, who really wasn't as formidable or as cavalier as he liked to pretend. She liked that Jordan Lynch, she thought suddenly. Liked him more than she could say.

Impatient with herself, she got up from her chair and started to clear away the empty dishes from the table. When she went into the villa she heard a foreign voice drifting towards her down the hallway, and for a moment she thought there was someone else in the house. Then she realised it was Jordan speaking fluent French on the phone.

She wondered to whom he was speaking at this hour of the night as she put the dishes into the dishwasher. For a moment she paused, listening to the deep, melodic flow of his conversation. She could only pick out the odd word, as her schoolgirl French wasn't that good. But it sounded wonderfully sexy. Impatient and annoyed with herself, she returned outside and poured herself the last of the coffee. She was like that moth, she thought as she watched it fly around and around the flame, occasionally making little darts towards it. Fascinated by him, yet terrified by the heat.

She blew the flame out and then, picking up her coffee-cup, walked down towards the pool. It looked very inviting; idly she dipped a toe in, and found the water silkily warm.

As Jordan returned outside he saw her beside the pool and stopped to watch her for a few moments. She probably didn't realise it but the lights from the water were shimmering behind her nightclothes so that he could see the outline of her body beneath. Unable to help himself, he ran his eyes up over her long legs and shapely curves and thought how beautiful she was. Like some Pre-Raphaelite painting with her long blonde hair flowing over her shoulders in glossy curls.

She dipped her toe into the water again and swirled it around.

'Go for a swim if you want,' he offered. 'The water is perfect. I have it regularly maintained.'

She spun around, surprised to find him standing on the patio, watching her. 'I didn't bring a swimming costume.'

'It doesn't matter. We're not overlooked out here.'

He watched her shrug awkwardly.

'If I were alone, maybe,' she murmured.

'Oh, I see.' He grinned. 'Well, if you're worried about me, don't be. I can already see everything there is to see.'

His eyes slipped down over her body again in a leisurely perusal. 'That night attire is completely see-through when you stand against the light.'

'I hope you're joking!' She moved very quickly away from the pool and he laughed at her consternation.

'I thought you were through getting embarrassed around me?' he asked mischievously.

'Yes, well, you continually sink to new lows,' she muttered, putting her empty coffee-cup down on the table. 'How long have you been standing there watching me?'

'Long enough.' He grinned. 'I don't know why you are so embarrassed. It's not as if I haven't seen everything you have anyway.'

She glared at him. 'If you were any kind of a gentleman you wouldn't bring that subject up, and you wouldn't have stood there watching me like…like some peeping Tom.'

'I'm only human, Charlie, and you have got a gorgeous body,' he said with a smile. 'And anyway, I never laid claim to being a gentleman.'

'You got something right anyway.'

She made to swing away from him but he reached out and caught her arm before she could move. 'Come and have a swim with me,' he invited huskily. 'I haven't got a swimming costume either.'

Dark hazel eyes held hers in a brazen challenge and suddenly her annoyance and embarrassment left her.

For a moment the thought of gliding through the water next to him, naked skin pressed against naked skin in the warm, silky heat, made her body burn with raw desire.

She wanted very much to throw caution away but, remembering how that moth had fluttered around the flame, she pulled away from him determinedly. 'That isn't a good idea, Jordan,' she murmured.

'Why not?'

'Because we are both tired and it's getting late…' She

broke off in panic as he reached out and flicked a light switch behind him, plunging the whole of the pool area into inky blackness. 'And we need to keep a clear head for tomorrow—'

'Are you always so sensible?'

The slightly mocking tone made her bristle inside. 'When I have to be.' She raised her eyes to his.

'You know I want you, don't you?' The whispered words set her blood on fire, as did the touch of his hand as he reached and brushed a stray strand of her hair away from her face.

She felt every nerve in her body tighten and tingle with awareness. Yes, she knew he wanted her, could see it in the predatory light in his eyes. She wanted him too; her heart was beating out of control against her chest and the longing to melt into his arms was so acute it was a deep ache.

'I…meant what I said earlier today, Jordan. I don't want to have a casual fling with you.' Her voice was unsteady as she fought against the traitorous weakness inside her.

'Because you're an old-fashioned girl?' His voice was husky and playful, and it set alarm bells ringing deep inside.

'Apart from all of that, we are on opposite sides of a divide.'

'We don't have to be on opposite sides, though, do we?' he murmured.

His eyes moved to her lips, and then slowly he lowered his head and kissed her. After a moment's hesitation she kissed him back. The sensation that flared between them was one of pure arousal, and suddenly she couldn't think straight any more; all she could do was wind her arms up and around his neck and hold on to him, give herself up to the hedonistic bliss of being so close to him.

He lowered his head and kissed her neck, then his fingers found the ties of her dressing gown and moved beneath to the warmth of her breasts, caressing the hardened nipples, making her catch her breath with ecstasy.

'You're so very beautiful,' he whispered.

'And you are very practised in the art of seduction.' Her voice held a tinge of grounded good sense and yet at the same time her lips were searching for his again.

His hands stroked down over her back and the dressing gown was pulled lower until she was freed from it. Then his hands curved around her narrow waist and his mouth trailed heated kisses over her naked shoulders.

'I thought you only wanted to go for a swim,' she reminded him huskily, rolling her head back as he kissed the sensitive hollow of her neck.

No one had ever kissed her the way Jordan did. The softness and the passion of his lips seemed to steal all rational thought away from her.

'To hell with the swim, let's just go upstairs.' His voice was laced with need and it echoed inside her, making her feel dizzy, as if she had been drinking.

She ran her fingers through his hair, loving the texture of it against her skin. Pressing herself closer, she reached to kiss him again. 'Yes, let's go upstairs,' she agreed huskily.

It was a shock when he suddenly swept her off her feet to carry her inside the house. There was something wildly exciting about being carried like this. She curved her arms around his neck and buried her face against his shirt, breathing in the scent of his cologne, loving the feeling of power about him. Her body felt alive with anticipation, with need, and with an excitement that only seemed heightened by her attempts to stem the flow of passion with words of caution. The knowledge that all she was doing tonight was playing with fire didn't stem her ardour—instead it seemed to be feeding it in some bizarre way. The danger and the excitement and the need were all entangled deep within her, making her want him more than ever.

They didn't turn the lights on in her bedroom; just a single shaft of moonlight fell softly from the window over the bed. It lent everything a strange, cool, silvery shade of unreality. As Charlotte leaned back against the pillows and watched Jordan undress she felt as if she wasn't really here at all, that it was all some wildly exhilarating dream.

She watched as his shirt was discarded, admiring the muscled perfection of his shoulders, the broad, powerful chest. As he sat on the edge of the bed beside her and began to unbuckle the belt of his jeans she felt the excitement inside suddenly turn to a kind of acute nervous apprehension. He had such a fabulous body and she remembered with vivid intensity how well he was able to use it.

'Jordan.' She reached out a hand and touched his arm.

He turned to look at her then and saw the apprehension clearly in her eyes. Leaving his jeans on, he moved to join her on the bed.

The flimsy silk of her nightdress might as well not have been there for all the difference it made. She was aware of every part of him in that moment, the strength of his body pressed close against hers.

He stroked her hair away from her face and looked deeply into her eyes. 'What's going through that mind of yours?' he asked softly.

'All the reasons why this isn't a good idea,' she whispered honestly.

'Sometimes it's a mistake to analyse things too deeply.'

'I should just relax and enjoy the moment, you mean.' Her voice was light. 'Not think about relationships at all.'

'There's nothing wrong with enjoying the moment you're in.'

They were so close that she could feel the vibrations of his voice against her chest.

He kissed her lips softly. It was passionate and compelling and it tore at something deep inside her. There was a sensation in the pit of her stomach as if someone had just pushed her off a cliff edge on a bungee rope.

Trouble was, she wanted more than just a moment in time with Jordan Lynch. She wanted much, much more.

I'm in love with this man, she thought hazily. Then, as the thought cleared and took a deeper hold on her consciousness, she felt herself freeze inside with fear.

'Jordan, this really isn't a good idea.' Her voice was breathless as if she had suddenly been running a race. She pushed him away from her but she needn't have tried to use force. He instantly moved back, allowing her the freedom to swing away from him and sit on the other side of the bed with her back to him.

'Why not?' His voice was very calm.

'Because…' She looked over at him. Jordan Lynch wasn't the kind of man to fall in love with, she told herself fiercely. Not unless you enjoyed having your heart broken. He was fickle when it came to women, enjoyed the chase and the thrill of lovemaking but didn't want the commitment. The only allegiance Jordan wanted was to the business.

'Because?' Jordan prompted her.

'It's just not a good idea, that's all.' Her voice was flat as she tried to close out the emotions that he stirred in her. 'And I'm worried about what's going to happen tomorrow with Dad and this money business.' Desperately, she tried to concentrate on the realities of their situation. 'I know you said you'd give him a few days to sort the problem out. But a few days might not be enough.'

'Oh, I see.'

She noticed the change in his tone from gently reasonable to cold and incisive.

'What do you see?' Her blonde hair swung around as she turned to look at him again.

'You are still in love with David, but you are not above using that beautiful body of yours as a bargaining chip after all.'

She flinched at the coldness of the words. And suddenly the implications of the way she had behaved struck her forcibly—her heat and passion one moment and now this. 'That's not true, Jordan.' Earnestly, she strove to set things straight. 'I told you this morning I wasn't like that and—'

'And you're just an old-fashioned girl?' His lips twisted wryly. 'You know, I believed that once, Charlie. But I don't think it's going to wash a second time.'

'Jordan!'

'Tell me, which is it that concerns you most—your father's fate? Or the shares you would like in the company?' He watched the colour flare under her skin. 'Just how much help are you hoping for?'

'I think you'd better leave,' she said tightly.

'Hit a nerve, have I?' He shook his head. 'You know, the really strange thing is that I still want you.' His eyes raked over her body before coming to rest on her face with a kind of deep intensity that made her body burn. 'Maybe because I recognise a kindred spirit, a person who knows what she wants and is not afraid to use whatever means she has at her disposal to get it.'

He reached out a hand and touched her face in a caress that was strangely at odds with the coolness of his words. His touch made her body heat up instantly and, to her humiliation, desire still stirred forcefully inside her. She flinched away from him, hating herself for the weakness. How he'd laugh if he knew the emotions that had really been driving her.

'OK, you're right.' She said the words shakily. 'I do want my rightful share of the family business and I do want you to go easy on my father.' She raised her eyes to his with a determination she was in reality far from feeling. 'And maybe I'm prepared to do anything it takes if you'll help.'

There was silence for a moment as Jordan studied her, dissected the words and then fitted them with the look of anguish in her eyes, the sudden pallor of her skin.

The anger that had driven him a second ago had been motivated by pure frustration. He wanted her…wanted her with a need he hadn't known in years. But he didn't want to hurt her and he was hurting her now. There was something about her demeanour that reminded him of a trapped animal, wounded but still determined to fight and protect what she loved.

'Your father is a lucky man to have you in his corner, Charlotte.' He said the words softly and then stood up.

She watched as he walked around the bed to stand with his back to her, looking out of the window.

For a long moment there was nothing said between them and Charlotte felt her nerves twisting with apprehension. She wished now that she hadn't tried to be clever, that she had never said those words. She wasn't in a strong enough bargaining position anyway; Jordan could have any woman he wanted. All this could do was make things worse. Charlotte opened her mouth to tell him she hadn't meant what she'd said, that she was tired…that she was frightened…anything that would extract her from the mess. But before she could speak he turned and looked at her again.

'OK, this is the deal.' He spoke coolly and decisively. 'If your father can't pay up but hands over the necessary amount of shares to me I won't prosecute—on two conditions.'

'And what are they?' Her heart was thumping painfully against her chest and her voice sounded as strained and as tense as she felt.

'One is that you stay working in the business for at least twelve months. We have a lot of contracts to finish, and tight deadlines. The last thing I need is you walking out right now.'

Her lips twisted wryly. She might have known that Jordan's main priority would be the business. 'And the second condition?' She angled her head up, wishing that the full force of the moonlight wasn't shining on her face, leaving him in darkness. She felt at enough of a disadvantage as it was and she really would have liked to be able to see his expression.

'That you make yourself available to me when I want you.' The words had a hard, uncompromising edge.

She felt her heart miss several beats. 'What do you mean by make myself available?'

'Just what I said. I think we need to work in closer unison, both in office hours and out of them.'

'You mean you want me to grace your bed whenever you feel like it?' She forced herself to ask the question.

'Why are you sounding so outraged, Charlotte?' Jordan's tone was quiet. 'Isn't that just what you were offering me a moment ago?'

'Jordan—I didn't mean to say that.' She stood up and moved a few steps closer to him. 'I'm under a lot of stress at the moment and—'

'And you really should think before you speak,' he cut across her firmly. He reached to touch her, smoothing her hair back from her face and studying her with quiet intensity. 'I have no intention of forcing you into my bed... that's not how I get my kicks, I can assure you.'

The touch of his hands made her senses cry out for him. Little did he realise that he wouldn't have to do that much forcing—she would willingly have gone into his arms even now.

OK, she wanted him; she admitted the truth to herself savagely—but she would never, ever tell him that. She had her pride. It was better to be branded cold-blooded than branded a fool, she told herself firmly. And she had enough sense to know that loving Jordan was a road to nowhere. He would respect her for wanting a share of the company, for wanting to help her father—but not for wanting him. He was a hard-headed businessman, not a sentimentalist.

'The deal is, you stay working for me and offer me as much of your time as I feel I need.' He moved away from her slightly so that they weren't touching. 'We can leave what happens between us in the bedroom as an optional extra.'

The coolness of his tone cut through her.

'Anyway, I don't expect an answer tonight. It's late and I suggest we both get some sleep. We'll talk tomorrow.'

Then he was gone, closing the door behind him with a quiet finality.

Charlotte sat back down on the bed and tried to get her head around what had just happened. It seemed she had brokered some kind of deal for her father and she felt relief at that…but at what personal cost to herself?

CHAPTER SEVEN

JORDAN knocked on her bedroom door. 'Charlotte, are you awake?'

There was no sound from inside the room. He knocked again and then pushed the door open.

Sunlight filtered through the windows, slanting over the bed where she was curled up, fast asleep. The white sheets were low, showing the flawless, creamy perfection of her skin, the soft curve of her breast. Her lashes were dark against her face, her lips softly parted. Her hair lay in golden curls over the pillows, framing her face. She looked warm and seductively inviting.

'Charlotte?' He trailed a finger down the smoothness of her cheek and then stroked a silky strand of hair from her face so that he could see her more clearly.

She looked vulnerable and fragile and it brought out an answering surge of protectiveness inside him that he hadn't felt in a long, long time. That was quite an act she had put on last night, he thought. How far would she really go to protect the people she loved?

He put the drink he had brought her down on the bedside table. 'Charlotte, you need to wake up,' he said softly.

She smiled in her sleep and stretched luxuriously. The movement showed the firm, creamy curve of her breast and suddenly he wanted to lie down beside her and take her into his arms, drown once again in the sweetness of her body. But then he had wanted to do that last night as well. It had taken all his self-control to leave this room.

Afterwards he had gone back outside and had swum as

many laps of the pool as possible in an effort to exhaust himself and get her out of his head. But it hadn't worked.

'Charlotte.' He raised his voice slightly.

The familiar voice trickled deliciously through her consciousness. For a moment she couldn't think where she was. Her eyes flicked open and met with Jordan's.

It took a moment for realisation to dawn on her and then she hastily pulled the sheet over herself.

'I've been trying to wake you for ages.'

'Have you? What time is it anyway?' She felt flustered and embarrassed as the full memory of last night flooded through her.

She remembered her ludicrous statement that she had only wanted to sleep with him to save her father and the business. Had he really believed that? She hoped he had, prayed that he didn't guess that somehow somewhere along the way she had fallen in love with him. That would be too humiliating to bear.

She flicked a nervous glance up at him and noticed he was fully dressed in lightweight fawn trousers and a cream polo shirt.

'It's seven forty-five.' He picked up the china mug from the table and handed it over to her. 'I wasn't sure if you were a tea person in the morning or a coffee. I took a guess at tea.'

'Thanks.' Self-consciously she sat up, struggling to keep the covers in place over her body before taking the cup from him. How could he talk about something as mundane as tea after what had transpired between them in here last night?

As she glanced nervously up at him he smiled and she wondered if that was a gleam of amusement playing around the sensual curve of his lips. He probably found this whole situation extremely entertaining. Even if he didn't prosecute her father, he was still in a very strong position to oust him from the company, and he was powerful enough and ruthless enough in business to do it.

Add to that the fact that he was probably congratulating himself on tying her into the business for a year, and all in all he had himself a nice little coup.

The thought was galling.

'So was I right or wrong?' he asked.

She looked up at him blankly, and then remembered what he had been saying. 'Oh, about the tea—yes, you were right. I drink tea in the morning.'

He nodded. 'You're not fully awake yet, are you? I'll leave you to come around in peace. Then we'll go and have breakfast in town.'

As the door closed behind him she put her tea down on the bedside table with a thump and rested her head back against the pillows. Breakfast! That was the last thing she wanted with the weight of anxiety that was hanging over her. All she wanted was to get today over with, find her father, face whatever problems had to be faced and forget those feelings for Jordan Lynch. Because he didn't deserve her love—he was cold-blooded and calculating.

She flung back the covers and got out of bed to head into the bathroom. Maybe she didn't really love Jordan at all, she told herself sharply as she stood under the full force of the shower jet. Maybe it was just a passing moment of insanity.

Maybe Jordan was right and she was on the rebound from David? She closed her eyes and thought about her feelings for David, but they seemed pale and insipid now next to the weight of feeling for Jordan.

Surely she wasn't so shallow that she imagined herself in love with him because they'd had great sex? She cast her mind back to that first night together, how close they had stood next to each other in his lounge, how he'd reached to touch her…the sensational, erotic, shivery feelings that had flowed through her when they'd kissed. The chemistry had been there between them even before they'd made love, she realised. But she'd been too blind to see it. Too blind—or too frightened by the intensity of feeling he seemed to stir up in her.

She remembered the first time she had ever met Jordan, when her father had brought him into her office to introduce them. She remembered looking up at him and how he'd smiled at her. That smile had seemed to ignite inside her into a million butterflies and she had immediately put up defensive barriers. She had watched from the safety of her relationship with David as a succession of beautiful women went through his life and she had told herself that she was doing the right thing keeping a distance from him. He was an unknown quantity…a dangerous entity…a heartache waiting to happen.

She had been right about all that, she told herself as she stepped out of the shower and dried herself briskly. Jordan was definitely dangerous: powerful, ambitious and sensually explosive.

Her hands trembled for a moment as she remembered the way he had kissed her by the pool last night, and the way he had made her feel so out of control.

Angrily she tried to shut the memory away. She couldn't deal with her feelings for Jordan right now. One thing at a time, and today she would face the problem of her father and the business.

Dressing in a bright pink sundress, she pinned her hair up and paid careful attention to her make-up. She felt quite satisfied with the results as she stepped back from the mirror and surveyed her reflection. At least she had managed to disguise the fact that it had taken hours before she finally slept last night and she looked her usual cool and capable self. Pity it was all a charade, she thought as she picked up her bag and headed out.

There was an open door along the corridor and her attention was caught and held by the view it afforded across lush greenery towards the bright azure blue of the Mediterranean. A few yachts were skipping over the waves, white sails fluttering in the breeze. The scenery was so captivating that she didn't realise for a moment that the room she was looking into had once been a child's bedroom. It was only as she turned to move on that she noticed the teddy bears on the bed, and the sight of them sent a shiver of sadness through her. This had obviously been Jordan's daughter's room.

She noticed the framed photographs on the dressing table—one of Natasha on her own, the other a family portrait: Natasha between her mother and father. Even from this distance she could see that Jordan's ex-wife was as beautiful as she had imagined. Her short dark hair was immaculately groomed and she had the chic look of a Parisian, high cheekbones, almond eyes and a wide, attractive smile.

A sound behind her in the corridor made her turn. Jordan was walking towards her. His eyes flicked from her to the open doorway she was standing in and she felt a pang of guilt as if she had been caught intruding on something intensely personal.

'I was just admiring the view,' she murmured as he reached her side.

He stretched past her and without a word closed the door. She noticed the shuttered expression in his eyes as he looked back at her. 'If you're ready, we should go.'

'Yes, of course.' Despite the coolness of his tone she had the impression that just glancing into that room was an unspeakable ordeal for him, and it made her heart go out to him. But before she could murmur any gentle words he moved away from her abruptly, leaving her feeling foolish for daring to think he might need her compassion.

'I rang the airline earlier; there's a flight back to London available at four-thirty this afternoon. I've booked us on it.'

She felt a pang of unease at the brisk, businesslike words. 'But what if Dad isn't there when we return to the house? It might take longer than just today to sort things out.'

'Charlotte, I have a business to run. The problem with your father will have to be sorted out today, one way or another.'

The decisive words made the knot of tension inside Charlotte tighten even further. Had Jordan changed his mind about the deal he had put to her last night? It seemed likely he had, otherwise surely he would have mentioned it again this morning. She followed him silently downstairs and out of the front door, trying desperately to gather the courage to bring the subject up.

The silence between them continued as they drove along the coast. The heat in the car was intense; Charlotte could feel it burning her through the fine cotton material of her dress, yet inside she was cold with fear.

If her father wasn't at the house this morning, would Jordan just call the police and be done with the problem?

She flicked an anxious look over at him, but his features seemed closed and guarded. It was impossible to tell what was going on in his mind.

As if sensing her eyes on him he spoke suddenly. 'I thought we'd have breakfast in St Tropez.'

'Jordan, I can't eat breakfast. I'm too wound up to eat anything.' Her voice came out in an agitated rush.

'Starving yourself isn't going to help anyone.' His voice was irritatingly calm. 'But, OK, we'll go straight to Port Grimaud.'

'Thanks.' She stared down at hands that were tightly

clenched in her lap. 'You will go easy on Dad, won't you?' she asked in a low tone.

He didn't answer her immediately and she glanced up as he slowed the car and then pulled it into the side of the road.

'Did you think about my proposition last night?'

'Yes, of course I did!' She looked into the depths of his hazel eyes and felt something inside her twist painfully at the remoteness of his tone and his manner.

'And?'

'And if the offer is still open then I accept your conditions.' She looked away from him out of the car window. 'I'll stay working in the business for a year.'

'Even if your father is no longer a part of the business?'

The calmly asked question made her anger return. 'I don't see why Dad should have to completely leave the company. OK, there is a lot of money outstanding from the business, but not that much!'

'The deal is that I don't prosecute and you stay on in the business, lending me your full co-operation, support and time in whatever capacity I feel I need it.' He cut across her with a dangerous quietness. 'That's the offer on the table, Charlotte—take it or leave it.'

She clenched her hands into tight fists of frustration. 'And you'll go easy on Dad.' She refused to back down completely. 'You'll treat him with deference.'

'Yes,' he nodded, 'of course I will. I've always liked your father—this isn't personal.'

She looked back at him, meeting his eyes steadily.

'Just business,' she said frigidly, hating the way he was able to dismiss all feelings, all sentiment when it came to the company.

'Just business,' he agreed.

'OK, then.' With the greatest of difficulty she kept her

voice light, tried to pretend that this agreement wasn't sticking in her throat. 'You've got yourself a deal.'

Charlotte noticed the gleam of satisfaction in his eyes and it aggravated her intensely, but she said nothing more. What else was there to say? The simple fact was that Jordan Lynch held all the cards in this game, and he knew it.

He put the car into gear and moved slowly back out into the road. 'Let's go and get this over with, then,' he said smoothly. 'The sooner we get back to normal, the better.'

Amen to that, Charlotte thought as she gazed out over the rows of vines in the fields and the wild poppies that decorated the roadsides.

Viewed in the daylight, Port Grimaud was every bit as select and beautiful as Charlotte had suspected. It was like a miniature Venice with canals and charming little hump-back bridges, each glimpsed view a true artist's delight. The houses were painted in ice-cream colours and they glinted fresh in the sunlight, their shutters open to the heat of the day. Most of them seemed to have their own private moorings, with yachts and small pleasure craft tied up alongside.

Despite the fact that Charlotte had intended not to speak to Jordan until she had to, she found herself remarking on how beautiful the surroundings were.

'Yes. It was the brainchild of an architect called Francois Spoerry and it's built on land reclaimed from the sea.'

'So it's relatively new, then? It looks as if it has always been here.'

'It's a designer's dream, isn't it? Everything about it is practically perfect. I think it was one of the projects that inspired me towards becoming an architect.' He slowed the car as they approached the house where they had called last night.

'Looks as if someone is at home anyway,' Jordan remarked, and she followed his gaze past the huge house with its pale pink walls and blue shutters towards the garage, noting that the doors were open and a blue car was parked inside.

Charlotte could hardly wait for the car to come to a standstill so that she could jump out.

As she hurried down the path someone else was coming around the other side of the house. She looked over and to her delight saw that it was her father.

'Dad!' she called to him and he turned and looked around at her, surprise clearly etched in his eyes.

'Charlotte! What on earth are you doing here?'

'Come to see you, of course.' As she walked over to him Charlotte noticed that he didn't look well. Simon McCann had always been a good-looking man who wore his age well, but now his face was gaunt and pale and he had lost a lot of weight in the weeks since she had seen him.

'Dad, are you OK?' Her voice catching with concern, she put her arms around him and gave him a hug.

'Well, I'm all the better for seeing you, sweetheart.' He hugged her back. Then over her shoulder his eyes connected with Jordan's.

'I'm glad to see you, too,' he said with quiet dignity. 'We have things to sort out.'

Jordan acknowledged the words with a nod.

As Charlotte moved back from her father Ruth walked around the side of the house. Her eyes widened as she saw Charlotte. 'I've been trying to ring you for days!'

'Well, I'm here now,' Charlotte said and noticed how the other woman looked over at Jordan with apprehension.

'Let's get inside.' Swiftly Ruth turned to lead them around the house towards the front door.

Her stepmother looked as immaculate as ever, Charlotte

noted. She was very slender and always perfectly groomed, her short blonde hair sat in its usual tidy style, and she was wearing casual white trousers and a white top that had a designer cut to them. It was only when Charlotte got close to her as she stepped inside the house that she could see there was something wrong. Despite the fact that Ruth had been in the sun for some weeks, her skin was white, and her eyes were heavy with anxiety.

'So how about a drink?' Ruth asked, her tone bright.

A drink was the last thing on Charlotte's list of requirements. She glanced around the house. It was like a Hollywood set, its huge rooms furnished with elegant style, and offering a view out across the bay of St Tropez that was truly spectacular.

'So what's been going on?' Charlotte cut directly to the point as she looked from her father to Ruth. It was the least probing of a number of questions running through her mind. But neither answered her.

'I'm sure you'd like a cool drink,' Ruth continued determinedly, giving a silent signal to Charlotte to follow her through to the kitchen.

Charlotte frowned and glanced again at her father. There was a frailty about him that she had never noticed before. 'Go and help Ruth with the drinks,' he said gently. 'I want a quiet word with Jordan.'

Charlotte's eyes darted to Jordan as she speculated about what the two men were going to say to each other. Whatever it was, she hoped Jordan was going to go easy on him; her father didn't look strong enough to take much in the way of confrontation.

As if he could read her thoughts, Jordan said soothingly, 'It's OK, Charlotte.'

'I hope so,' she murmured, turning to leave them.

Ruth was waiting for her in the kitchen. She was leaning against the blue kitchen counter, her arms tightly crossed in front of her, her whole body language screaming defence. 'Are you angry with me over this business?' she asked as soon as Charlotte stepped through the door.

Charlotte's eyes flicked over her stepmother and noticed that behind that wary expression she looked tired.

'No, I'm not angry,' Charlotte said quietly. 'Just puzzled.'

'Oh!' Ruth unfolded her arms and the look of relief in her blue eyes was immense. 'Thank God for that. I don't think I could have dealt with any more anger. I've had enough from your father.'

'So what's all this about?' Charlotte asked crisply. 'Why is there money missing from the company accounts?'

Ruth looked miserable. 'It's all a terrible mistake, Charlotte, and I'm so sorry… I can't tell you how sorry I am.' She turned and opened a cupboard and took out a bottle of Scotch. 'I could do with something stronger than a soft drink. What about you?'

'No, I don't want anything.' Charlotte sat down on one of the stools at the breakfast bar and tried to be patient, even though curiosity was eating her away.

'Is Jordan furious about the money?' Ruth asked in a strained whisper.

'I don't think he's too happy,' Charlotte said. 'But he's a businessman, Ruth; what can you expect? It was a lot of money. And it wasn't even so much that as the way it was done.'

Ruth nodded and poured herself a generous measure from the bottle of whisky. 'I hope he isn't too hard on your father, Charlie,' she said anxiously. 'This was all my fault, not his.'

Charlotte glanced around towards the lounge and saw that the two men had stepped outside onto the deck.

They didn't seem to be talking at all at the moment, she noticed. Her father was leaning on the rail, staring down into the sea as if deep in thought. Jordan was standing next to him, glancing out across the bay as if he was just admiring the view.

Charlotte turned her attention back to Ruth. 'So are you going to tell me what all this is about?'

Ruth took a deep swallow of her drink. 'He told me not to tell you this,' she murmured. 'Made me swear to it. But I can't carry this worry all on my own, Charlotte. I've tried, and look at the mess I've got into.'

'What worry? What is it you aren't supposed to tell me?'

'Your father has a heart condition.' Ruth said the words softly. 'The doctors have told him that if he doesn't give work up he could be dead within the year.' She watched Charlotte's face drain of colour. 'That was seven months ago,' she stated grimly. 'Since then I've begged and pleaded with him to retire. But he wouldn't listen. Then I managed to get him out here for this holiday after Jordan had mentioned casually how beautiful the Côte d'Azur was.

'We rented this place and then discovered it was up for sale. Simon loved it, and toyed with the idea of buying it. Said that, just for me, he would give work up as the specialist had advised and we'd live out here and enjoy his early retirement.' Her voice cracked. 'And then at the last minute he changed his mind. Said that leaving the business would be letting everybody down. I begged him and pleaded with him…' Her eyes filled with tears suddenly. 'But he wouldn't listen.' Fiercely Ruth rubbed the tears away from her eyes.

'So?' Charlotte prompted softly.

'Other buyers came on the scene, and I was panicking, Charlotte. Your father wouldn't budge. So in desperation I used the money from the business account. I had the access code and I knew what to do.'

'I can't believe you did that,' Charlotte said in a hushed tone.

'It was only supposed to be an interim measure! I thought your father would have the funds to cover the money I took. After all, he was thinking of buying the place up to a few weeks ago.' Ruth ran her hand through her blonde hair in agitation. 'How was I to know that the reason he was suddenly against the purchase was the fact that he'd have to sell some shares in the company to afford it? He never told me that…but of course he wouldn't dare because he knows I want him to give the business up completely, never mind just a small part. The place is killing him, Charlotte!'

Charlotte was stunned into silence.

Ruth caught her eye. 'I was desperate,' she said firmly. 'Please don't look at me like that! There has been a marked improvement in your father's health since he has been out here. He even agreed to stay longer than we'd originally planned. I thought, if I could ease him over here with the purchase of the house, he'd finally let go of the business and realise how much he has to lose by ignoring the doctor's orders.' Ruth glared at her through a mist of tears. 'Under the circumstances, were my actions really so wrong? Simon is older than me anyway. I knew when I married him that we might not have as long together as some couples…and I want time with him… I love him.'

'I know.' Charlotte heard the real anguish in the other woman's tone and got up off the stool to go and put her arms around her. 'I know you love him.'

For a while the two women just stood there together, holding each other. Charlotte couldn't bear to think of her father being so ill. That he might die. It put all the worries about money and business very firmly into perspective.

'I've put everything in his name, you know, Charlotte.

I haven't done anything that wasn't in your father's best interests.'

'I don't doubt your intentions, Ruth,' Charlotte said as she pulled away. 'I just wish you had told me about this sooner. I'd have helped to try and talk him into retiring.'

Ruth shook her head. 'You know what he's like…so damn stubborn. The more you try to talk him around, the more likely he is to go completely the other way. That's why I ended up taking things into my own hands. I realise now what a mistake it was.

'When I told him a few days ago what I had done, he nearly had apoplexy. Told me that I was a bloody fool and he couldn't put the money back because he didn't have it! I can't tell you how shocked I was, Charlotte. I thought it would just be a simple matter of transferring funds from one account to another. And I thought it could be done within a matter of minutes with the electronic banking system that we have in place. But apparently Simon has made bad investments in shares…lost a considerable amount of his savings. Unfortunately he didn't deign to tell me about it.' Her voice hardened as she turned to take another drink from her glass.

'But the situation is salvageable.' Ruth talked with her back to Charlotte now. 'I rang Jordan a few days ago and asked him in a round-about way if he would be willing and able to buy some of your father's shares in the business. Jordan said categorically that he would, that in fact he'd like to buy Simon out completely.'

'But Dad doesn't want to sell?'

Ruth turned then and her eyes were heavy with regret. 'No, he doesn't. He's been running around for the last three…no, four days, trying to raise the money to pay the debt off so that he doesn't have to touch his shares and he doesn't have to leave the business. Last night he went to see the people who were bidding against us for this house, offered it to them for fractionally less than I paid. Now, how crazy is that?' For a second her voice wobbled precariously and she looked close to tears again. 'I feel such a fool, Charlotte, but worse, I feel that your father doesn't love me at all. Because if he did he wouldn't want to go back to work. He'd want to take things easier, if not for himself then for me.'

'You've got to understand, Ruth, that Dad is a very proud man,' Charlotte said softly. 'For one thing, he won't want to lose face in front of Jordan—'

'Oh, you're right there. We both thought that we'd have a few more days before Jordan found out about this. The audits were due in next week, not last week. Simon was hell-bent on having the money back by then.'

'Yeah, well, you reckoned without Jordan's eagle eye. Nothing escapes his attention in that office. Actually, he's like Dad in a lot of ways, now I think about it.'

'Probably why the two of them get on so well.' Ruth sniffed loudly and reached for a tissue. 'What am I going to do, Charlotte? Do you think Jordan will bail us out?'

'If Dad is prepared to compromise, I think he might.' Charlotte thought about the deal she had cut with Jordan last night. 'In fact, I know he will.'

Tears of relief streamed down Ruth's face. 'I always liked Jordan, he's a pretty good bloke really.'

'He has his moments,' Charlotte muttered. She glanced outside again; the two men were deep in conversation now. Nervously she hoped that Jordan was keeping his end of their deal, and was playing everything gently down.

'I hope he's calming Simon down a bit…' Ruth said as she followed Charlotte's gaze. 'We are barely on speaking terms at the moment.'

'Yes, I hope he is too,' Charlotte murmured. 'Dad really doesn't look well.'

'Which is why he needs to retire,' Ruth said firmly. 'He

should be selling our apartment in London, not this house. He needs to get completely away from the office.'

'I agree.' Charlotte looked back around at the other woman. 'But we can't force him into leaving the business. At the end of the day, it's going to have to be his decision. You've got to understand, Ruth, the business has been everything to him for years. After Mum died he buried himself in it completely. That's one of the reasons Jen and I were so delighted when he married you—he actually does take time off now, which is more than he ever did before. But it will be very difficult for him to let go entirely, especially as it's been a family concern for so long. We're going to have to handle this very carefully.'

'Actually, the problem has been solved.' Jordan appeared in the doorway behind them and they both turned around in surprise.

'Simon wants to know if you'll bring out the bottle of champagne from the fridge, and four glasses.'

'Champagne?' Ruth sounded bewildered. 'Are we celebrating something?'

'Yes. The fact that you have acquired a full-time husband and I have acquired a business.'

The decisive words made consternation flood through Charlotte. 'What do you mean? What's happened?'

'I mean that we've talked the matter through and, in view of Simon's health, we have decided that it's best that I buy him out. This way your father can enjoy a comfortable and well-deserved retirement.'

There was a stunned silence for a few moments.

Charlotte frowned. 'Ruth told me he was determined to go back to the business.'

'Well, he's changed his mind.'

Charlotte met the dark strength of Jordan's eyes and felt a wave of fury at the nonchalant way he said those words. She didn't believe for one moment that her father had changed his mind so easily and so quickly of his own free will.

'Well, this is good news for me,' Ruth said with a sigh of relief. 'Anything that means Simon won't be going into that office is a good thing.'

Simon came into the room behind Jordan. He gave his wife a shaky smile. 'Well, you've got your wish—you're going to have me under your feet for twenty-four hours a day, Ruth. I just hope you're not going to regret it.'

'So my neck isn't to be put on a chopping block after all,' Ruth commented wryly.

'Not this week anyway,' Simon grinned, in a shadowy attempt at his once robust humour.

'Hold on a minute, Dad.' Charlotte cut across the conversation swiftly. 'Everything is moving just a little too quickly here. Are you happy about this?'

'The business will always be of interest to me…but…' Simon glanced over at Ruth. 'Maybe Jordan and Ruth are right. Some things in life are more important than work. I'm sorry, Ruth, I know I've put you under a lot of strain these last few months. And you're right, my health and our relationship should come first. I intend to put things right.'

Charlotte watched as he moved to take Ruth into his arms. Then she turned and stepped past Jordan to head outside and give them some privacy.

It was hot on the deck; even the breeze that swept across the bay did little to reduce the temperature. Charlotte leaned against the rail and looked out to sea. The town of St Tropez shimmered in the distance, a terracotta blaze of colour between the green of the mountains and the blue of the Med.

Jordan came to stand next to her and suddenly the heat around them was nothing to the heat of the temper inside her.

'Well, you've got control of the business at last.' She practically hissed the words. 'Congratulations.'

'I'd like to say thanks, but your tone of voice doesn't seem to lend itself to the word.'

His lazy indifference was the last straw. 'You really are a bastard, Jordan Lynch.' She swung to face him, her eyes blazing into his. 'A complete bastard.'

'That's not a very nice way to speak to your boss, Charlotte,' he said drolly.

'I don't give a toss how I speak to you. I think you're contemptible. You've strong-armed him into this, haven't you?' she continued furiously. 'Blackmailed him into selling out to you completely, just as you've blackmailed me into staying on at the business.'

'I haven't blackmailed Simon into anything.'

'You must think I'm totally naïve if you imagine I'd believe that.' She shook her head. 'I know how you operate, Jordan. I've seen you in action. And you disgust me.'

'Really? Am I to take it, then, that our deal is off?'

The quietly spoken words caused a ripple of cool in the heat of her anger. 'If I say our deal is off you'll call the police in.'

Jordan shrugged. 'So the ball is in your court.'

Charlotte's eyes shimmered like cool chips of green malachite in the heat of the day.

'If it makes you feel any better your father is retaining ten per cent of his shares, so you will have something of the family business one day.'

'Gosh! You've allowed him to keep ten per cent. How big of you!' she grated derisively. 'How magnanimous. Shall I kiss your feet now or later?'

'Later will do.' Humour danced in Jordan's eyes for a second. 'I like a bit of privacy when people are kissing my feet.'

'Laugh all you like, Jordan. But you can't exploit people the way you do and get away with it.'

'I can assure you I haven't got away with anything. Unravelling the mess your father was in and buying out the majority of his shares has not come cheap.' Jordan looked over towards the doorway as her father and Ruth came out onto the deck to join them, bringing a tray with the champagne.

'And I suggest if you don't want all the good work that has been done today to go to waste, you paste a smile on your face and wish your father well in his retirement.'

CHAPTER EIGHT

IT WAS early evening as they got into a taxi outside Heathrow Airport.

'Would you mind dropping me off at Jennifer's house first?' Charlotte asked Jordan as they settled themselves back in the seats.

'No problem,' Jordan agreed and gave the instructions to the driver.

Then he closed the glass partition and sat back beside her. The same tense silence that had accompanied them since leaving her father and Ruth enveloped them again.

Charlotte stared out at the grey and gloomy London weather and told herself that if she never spoke to Jordan Lynch again, it wouldn't be a moment too soon. And the notion that she might be in love with him seemed absurd now; in fact she was starting to believe that in reality she might actually hate him.

How she had managed to keep up a cheerful front for her father and Ruth she didn't know, because inside she had been seething. And her father's graceful acceptance of the situation had just made her feel worse. He had behaved like a real gentleman towards Jordan, but inside he must have been devastated. After all those years of building up the business it must have been heartbreaking to have it taken forcibly away from him with the threat of prosecution.

Jordan picked up his briefcase from the floor now and his sleeve brushed against hers. She moved further away from him across the seat as if his touch might contaminate her.

They hadn't stayed very long with her father because Jordan had said he'd some business to take care of in St Tropez. What that business was she had no idea; he hadn't told her and she hadn't asked. She'd wandered around the crowded streets alone, looking into the windows of the smart boutiques and admiring the luxury yachts lined up along the harbour, trying to calm down before meeting him back at the designated café. There was no point arguing with him, she had told herself firmly. She couldn't win.

They had ordered lunch at the café. Charlotte could still see the colourful blaze of the day as the heat shimmered over the smart, sophisticated crowds, the artists on the quay, the boats in the bay. She had studied it all quite intently, determined not even to glance over at Jordan.

It had been the same on the aircraft on the way home. She had totally ignored him and concentrated instead on the work she had brought with her.

Of course, Jordan didn't care. He had actually had the audacity to say he was glad they had got off to such a good start with her demonstrating her commitment to work.

She watched now out of the corner of her eye as he took out his mobile phone and started to make a few calls. They were all work-related, checking appointments with builders and other contractors and finally ringing his secretary Laura to tell her he'd be into the office in the morning.

Charlotte listened to the friendly banter and it just irritated her further. Strange how he could sound like such a nice guy when in reality he was a barracuda.

'Everything seems to be in order in the office,' he remarked as he ended the call. 'In fact they've had a very productive day by the sounds of it.'

'More money in the coffers. You must be overjoyed,' Charlotte replied drily. 'I know how important that is to you.'

'How long are you going to keep this up?' he asked suddenly.

'I don't know what you are talking about.' She kept her face averted from him.

'I'm talking about the stony silences broken only by the occasional barbed remark, as well you know.'

She looked around at him then. 'We had a deal. You said you'd go easy on Dad; you said you'd treat him with deference.'

'And I did. The matter is resolved, Charlotte, so just leave it.'

'The matter isn't resolved as far as I'm concerned. My father is a gravely ill man and you took advantage of that.'

'Yes, your father is gravely ill and he needs to retire. You need to face facts, Charlie—it was that or a premature death. Maybe you should think about that before criticising me.'

She bit down on the softness of her lips and looked away from him again. The truth was she couldn't bear to think too deeply about that at all.

'The right outcome has been reached for all concerned today,' Jordan continued in a more gentle tone.

'Now it just remains for me to break the news to Jen,' Charlotte said quietly.

'Tell Jen what exactly?'

'What's the matter, frightened I might tell her how you ruthlessly grabbed the family business?' For a moment her voice was scathing again, then she dropped the tone. 'Well, you needn't worry. I was referring to the fact that I'm going to have to tell her something about Dad's health.'

'He was quite adamant that you shouldn't say anything to her,' Jordan reminded her.

'I know, but it's not really fair, is it? If something should happen to him—and, God willing, it won't and he'll be fine now—but if the worst should happen it would be a terrible shock for Jen. I need to say something to prepare her.'

The taxi turned into the street where her sister lived and started to slow down. 'Anywhere along here is fine,' she called to the driver and started to collect her belongings.

Jordan reached to help her with her bag and their hands connected on the handle. The contact sent a dart of awareness rushing through Charlotte's body and she swiftly pulled away. 'I can manage, thank you,' she said stiffly.

But he didn't release the bag and, as the taxi stopped and she alighted, he still didn't hand it over to her, but got out on the pavement beside her.

'Well, goodbye, Jordan; I'll see you in the office tomorrow.' Her voice was coolly dismissive.

'Your car is still here from Sunday, isn't it?' he said, totally ignoring her words and glancing down the road to where it was parked.

'Yes...'

'Good. You can give me a lift home.'

His arrogance really grated on her but there seemed little she could do because he was already getting his overnight case from the taxi and paying the driver.

'You must be really worried about what I'm going to tell Jen,' she muttered as he walked with her up to the front door.

'I'm not worried at all.' Jordan stated with cool confidence.

'It would be a bit of a blow to your ego if I was to dent your ''Mr Nice Guy'' image, though, wouldn't it?'

'Go ahead, be my guest.'

She really wanted to ruffle that smug confidence of his, itched to march in to Jennifer's and tell her exactly what had been going on.

But, as the door opened and Harriet flung herself out to greet them, she knew that doing such a thing wasn't really an option. Jordan was too cold-blooded to care what she said and it would only upset Jennifer.

'Uncle Jordan's here! And Auntie Charlie!' Harriet called out to her mother in loud, excited tones, hardly able to wait for Jordan to put down the bags in the hallway before she pulled at his sleeve and he swung her up into his arms, making her giggle helplessly.

'Gosh, you're back already!' Jen appeared in the kitchen doorway and came over to greet them with a kiss. 'We didn't expect you for at least another four days.'

'Call of the office,' Jordan said with a grin. 'Otherwise we might have been tempted to stay.'

'Come on through—I've just put the kettle on.' Jennifer led the way into the kitchen. It was warm and smelt of coffee.

Was it really only two days since she'd last been here? Charlotte thought as she glanced across the kitchen table at Jordan. So much had happened in the interim that it felt like a month ago.

'Did you have a nice time?' Jen asked as she placed two china mugs of coffee before them.

Charlotte carefully avoided Jordan's gaze. 'It wasn't really a pleasure trip—we went to see Dad. There are a few things I need to tell you.'

Harriet was skipping around the table. 'I was painting at school today, Uncle Jordan,' she said happily. 'I painted a picture for you.'

'For me?' Jordan said with a grin.

Harriet nodded. 'I'll go and get it.'

In the ensuing silence as Harriet left the room Charlotte started to tell Jennifer about their father's health. Jordan noticed how carefully she chose her words, playing down the situation enough so that it didn't come as such a terrible shock and answering Jennifer's questions with a quiet calm.

There was only the slightest edge to her tone as she went on to tell her sister that Jordan would now be running the company while their father took things easy in France.

Jordan smiled at her as their eyes connected briefly across the table and for a second her composure slipped and he saw the gleam of fury in her green eyes.

Harriet came running back into the kitchen at that moment, breaking the silent communication between them across the table.

'Here, Uncle Jordan, here's my picture.' She shoved the piece of paper in front of him proudly.

'My goodness, your daughter has hidden talents, Jen,' he said with a grin. 'She could go and take a pitch on the quay at St Tropez.'

Jennifer laughed.

'Show Auntie Charlie,' Harriet urged him excitedly.

Jordan made the sound of a roll of drums with one hand on the table and then turned the masterpiece for Charlotte's inspection.

It was a jazzy impression of blue sea and waving palm trees with two matchstick people, arms entwined, faces close together, wearing heavy black sunglasses and manic grins.

'That's you, Auntie Charlie,' Harriet said, pointing to the figure with wild yellow hair.

Charlotte had to smile. 'It's wonderful, darling.'

'Hasn't she captured the mood perfectly?' Jordan said with a gleam of amusement in his dark eyes. 'And she tells me she has never been to France.'

'That's true, isn't it, Mummy? I've never been to France.'

'No, darling, but maybe it won't be long before you do go because Grandad and Granny Ruth have bought a beautiful house out there.'

'Wow! What colour is it?'

'Pink,' Jordan said. 'And the sea is just outside the windows.'

'Great! I'll go and draw a picture.'

As Harriet hurried off her mother called after her, 'Try not to wake the baby, please, darling.'

Jennifer smiled over at Jordan. 'So, congratulations about the business.'

'Thanks. It's a shame I'll be taking over under such trying circumstances for your father. He did a good job over the years building up the company.' Jordan spoke to Jen but his eyes were on Charlotte. 'I have always respected Simon.'

Hypocrite, Charlotte thought angrily.

'Well, you've got Charlotte.' Jennifer grinned.

'For the time being.' Charlotte couldn't resist muttering the words in an undertone and she knew Jordan had heard her by the way his eyes narrowed slightly with displeasure.

'Dad always used to say she was his right-hand man,' Jennifer continued, her attention distracted by the cries from the baby monitor that was plugged in beside them. 'I had better go and see to her. Why don't you two stay for supper? Steve will be home soon.'

As Charlotte opened her mouth to refuse Jordan spoke for her. 'Thanks for the offer, but we've got to get off. Charlie and I still have things we need to discuss before going into the office tomorrow.'

Was there no end to the man's arrogance? Charlotte thought. He seemed to be taking her over and she hated it. What did he want to discuss with her anyway? she wondered. Or was that just an excuse to get her out of the front door before she said anything else about his so-called 'respect' for their father?

'Thanks for the coffee, Jen.'

'You're welcome. I'll just go and pick Nicole up; I won't be a moment.'

'Nicole?' Charlotte looked across at her sister and smiled as they walked out into the hallway. 'You've had a breakthrough with choosing a name, then?'

'Yes, we've compromised,' Jennifer said happily. 'We'll give her Estelle as a second name, after Steve's mother.'

'That's really pretty.'

'Yes, I think so.' Jennifer started to hurry up the stairs. 'Hold on a moment—I'll just lift her up…won't be long.'

'Are you going home?' Harriet asked dolefully as she popped her head out from the lounge. 'I haven't finished my picture yet.'

'We'll see it next time,' Jordan smiled. 'And there's a little something here for you from France.' He opened the side flap of his briefcase and brought out a small gift-wrapped present with a gold sticker saying St Tropez on it. 'Now, be careful how you open it, there is a little pet inside so you don't want him to escape.'

Harriet's eyes lit up with excitement. 'Thank you,' she said, tearing open the paper.

Charlotte watched with interest as she lifted out a small box covered in yellow and green traditional Provence fabric.

'What is it, Uncle Jordan?' she asked in anticipation.

'Open it up and see.'

Gingerly she opened the lid, her eyes widening in surprise at the sound that issued forth immediately. It was the singing hum of a cicada and inside a little black insect was bobbing up and down in a little dance.

Harriet slapped the lid back down. 'Is it real?' she asked, her face a picture of animation.

'No, it's just pretend. But it will sing for you every time you open up the lid.'

She opened it again to peep inside and once more the sweet sound filled the air.

'That's cool! Wait until I show my friends at school.'

Jen laughed as she returned down the stairs with Nicole in her arms. 'We can all listen to that and pretend we're in the tropics.'

For Charlotte the sound brought back the vivid memory of Jordan's villa, and the way Jordan had held her in his arms that night on the terrace before going upstairs. The memory was so disturbingly intense that she felt her whole body heating up from it.

'He's such a nice guy, isn't he?' Jen said in a low tone as he walked ahead of them to put the luggage in the boot of Charlotte's car. 'I'm so glad that you're hitting it off so well.'

Charlotte made no reply. There was a part of her that was touched that Jordan had remembered to bring Harriet a present…it confused her, threw all the brutal words she had been silently aiming at him all day into muddled disarray.

He was a ruthless, blackmailing swine, she tried to remind herself, but, as she watched him grin in a good-natured way at Harriet as she jumped up and down beside him, the words lacked the fire that they should have had.

'Right. I'll speak to you tomorrow, Jen.' Charlotte busied herself opening the boot for Jordan. She couldn't allow herself to be taken in by him, she told herself fiercely, not when she knew the truth. 'And Dad said he'd phone you, and not to worry, he'll be back in plenty of time for the christening.'

'Do you want me to drive?' Jordan offered as he put the bags into the car.

'No, thank you.' She moved away from him and slipped behind the wheel of her car. At least if she was driving she felt as if she had some control over the situation, however flimsy that might be.

'That went all right,' Jordan murmured as they waved goodbye to Jennifer and pulled away down the road.

'Yes, your "Mr Nice Guy" image is still intact,' Charlotte murmured.

'But not with you,' Jordan said sardonically.

'I know the real Jordan Lynch, remember.'

'You know, I'm starting to think that you quite like telling yourself that I'm a heartless bastard. It's like a convenient safety barrier that you can hide behind, isn't it? Saves you facing up to the fact that there is a very strong sexual chemistry between us.'

'There is no such thing!' That remark sent her blood pressure shooting up. 'The only feelings I have for you are ones of…of distaste.'

'You're lying, Charlotte, you know it, and so do I.'

The calm words made heat frizzle inside her. 'All I know is that you are arrogant and cold-blooded.'

'You didn't think I was cold-blooded the night we made love. In fact, as I remember it you were very enthusiastic…very responsive.'

'That night was a mistake.' Charlotte's hands gripped the steering wheel so tightly that her knuckles gleamed white.

'And when we were at the villa you kissed me with equal passion…you came on to me as much as I came on to you.'

'You know why I did that.' She glared at him furiously. 'I was worried about my father and…and…'

'And you made me an offer. Yes, I remember.' He smiled. 'And we agreed terms.'

The words caused extreme consternation inside her. What did he mean by that? Was he telling her that he intended taking her up on that offer? Would he be calling in payment in kind?

A silence fell between them again but it wasn't the cool one that had been there all day. This seemed to be laced with a raw, intense heat.

She tried to pretend that she wasn't conscious of the way he was watching her now. Tried not to think about that offer, or their kisses, or the disconcerting memory of how much she had really wanted him last night.

'Anyway, emotionally I'm still smarting over David.' She drew her ex's name like a sword to protect herself, but even as she said the words she knew they weren't true.

'Even though he slept with your best friend?'

'She wasn't my best friend…she was just *a* friend.' The cool words caused havoc inside Charlotte. 'And how the hell do you know that?' She swung her eyes away from the road to glare at him.

'It's common knowledge around the office.' Jordan shrugged. 'And do you think you could keep your eyes on the road? I know it's quiet out here but I want to arrive back in London in one piece.'

Charlotte glowered at the road ahead. 'So when you asked me at my apartment what David was apologising for, you already knew?'

'Yes, but I was interested in your side of the story. I just wondered how you felt about him now,' he said softly. 'Obviously the subject is still very raw. But he's not worth being upset over.'

'I'm not upset with him. I'm upset with you for gossiping about me in the office.'

'I overheard it, that's all,' he said coolly. 'I haven't got time for gossip in the office.'

The offhand remark made her even more annoyed. 'You've got time to gossip when it suits you.' She couldn't resist the sideways swipe. 'I heard you telling someone on the phone about how you'd slept with me.'

He frowned at that. 'I have never discussed my private affairs with anyone.' His voice sounded ominously cold now.

'I heard you,' Charlotte insisted firmly. 'It was the

morning after we slept together and you were laughing and saying how you'd invited me in for coffee and got carried away...'

She began to wish she hadn't started this subject now. It was far too embarrassing and the way Jordan was watching her through those narrowed dark eyes was very disconcerting.

'I was talking to your sister,' he said coolly.

She frowned. 'My sister?'

'She phoned to invite me for Sunday lunch. And strangely she already seemed to know what had happened between us because she was teasing me quite unmercifully.'

He watched the consternation in her expression and grinned suddenly. 'So if we're apportioning blame for gossiping here, it seems that you are the guilty one, not me.'

'But I thought—'

'Yes, it's clear what you thought,' Jordan cut across her flatly. 'But I can assure you, Charlotte, I have never got my kicks in that way.'

She flinched. 'Yes, well, you can't really blame me for thinking what I did,' she mumbled. 'You do have a bit of a reputation where women are concerned.'

'Maybe.' He shrugged and conceded the point. 'I decided the day my divorce came through that I wasn't going to fall in love again. And a lot of women have passed through my life. But that doesn't mean I haven't treated them with respect.'

She wanted to make some kind of sarcastic reply to that, but found she couldn't. Jordan must have been hurt badly by the divorce. Maybe he still had feelings for his ex-wife even now? Not that she cared, she told herself fiercely. She couldn't give one fig about Jordan's love life.

'Can you really forgive David for the affair?' Jordan said into the silence. 'And forget about it totally?'

'It wasn't an affair, it was one night.' Her eyes shimmered emphatically as she glanced back over at him. 'You and I of all people should know that doesn't mean anything.'

'Doesn't lessen the pain of betrayal, though, does it?' Jordan said calmly.

'No.' She looked away from him.

But the strange thing was that she was more upset about her friend Linda's betrayal than David's.

They were heading away from the countryside now and the sun was trying to get out behind the greyness of the clouds in a final burst of colour before it set for the evening.

Charlotte paused at a crossroads, wondering which way would be the quickest. She needed to dump Jordan outside his apartment as speedily as possible. She couldn't think straight with him around.

'The road to the left would be best,' Jordan suggested.

'I'm not sure that's the quickest way for you.'

'No, but it's the quickest route back to your place.'

She looked over and met his eyes and the consternation inside her seemed to increase a hundredfold.

'There's a taxi rank around the corner from your place,' he said calmly. 'I'll take one from there; it will save you having to drive across the city.'

Charlotte hesitated for a moment. What he'd suggested made sense. With a bit of luck, and if she put her foot down, she might be free of Jordan Lynch very soon. She turned the car left with a feeling almost of relief. As soon as she was away from his close proximity she would be able to clear her head, think about things objectively—something she seemed incapable of doing around him.

However if she had thought that losing Jordan would be a straightforward and easy manoeuvre she was wrong.

When they finally pulled up outside her apartment he insisted on carrying her bags inside for her.

'OK, thank you very much.' She stood by the open front door as he put the bags down, tried to pretend that she was busy flicking through the mail she had lifted from the floor. But in reality she was trying to make it clear to him that she was waiting for him to leave.

As he walked back over towards her she hoped he was just going to say goodbye and walk out, but to her annoyance he took hold of the door and closed it.

'I thought you were leaving.'

'We've got unfinished business.'

'What kind of unfinished business?' She felt her nerves spiralling as he reached and took the envelopes from her hand, placing them down on the hall table beside them. He was standing very close to her…too close for comfort, and she took a step back, but there was nowhere for her to go. She was pressed against the wall.

'Well, for one thing we need to talk about where we go from here.'

'You go home and I give a big sigh of relief.' She met his eyes and tried to pretend that she was completely impervious to him.

'You see, this is the problem; this attitude of yours isn't very helpful, Charlie. We've got to work together tomorrow and I don't see that it's going to be a very successful union with you glaring at me all the time as if I'm public enemy number one.'

'In my eyes you *are* public enemy number one. You might have bought the business, Jordan, but I'm not part of the fixtures and fittings. I might have to work for you, but I don't have to like you.'

'Such tough words.' He leaned one hand on the wall next to her and bent closer. 'So why is it, do you think, that your lips tell me quite a different story?' She noticed the way his eyes were lingering on her lips and the look made her tremble inside, but not with fear, or distaste or any of the emotions that should have been shaking her; this was desire, pure and powerful.

'I don't know what you are talking about.' Her voice was huskily unsteady now.

'I think you do.' He leaned even closer and his lips were a whisper from hers now. 'I think you are well aware of what I'm talking about.'

She was aware of the familiar scent of his aftershave, delicious and provocative, the powerful body was just inches from hers and weakly she felt drawn to it as if by some magnetising force.

She clenched her hands into tight fists at her sides, determined to fight the traitorous feelings. 'All I'm aware of is how much I hate you,' she maintained stubbornly.

'Hate is such a strong emotion.' He leaned down and stroked a finger over her cheek in a sensual caress. 'Shall we put those words to the test?'

'Jordan, I—' Anything else she might have said was cut off abruptly as his lips moved to cover hers.

He kissed her forcefully, and with such passion that she felt the need for him exploding inside her like a firecracker. But she was determined not to respond to him; she held herself rigidly still, her hands immobile, clenched by her sides.

Then the kisses softened, became seductively slower, compellingly fervent, and without thinking she reached up to rest her hands on his shoulders. Then she kissed him back. She couldn't help herself; the feeling of need inside her was suddenly too great to ignore, the urgent desire he conjured up too powerful.

'That's better.' His tone was husky and filled with a lazy satisfaction, and even as she registered it and told herself not to feed his ego any further but to pull away she found she couldn't. Instead she leaned closer, matching his kisses passionately, loving the thrill of his body pressed against hers.

She felt his hands moving with possessive ease over her and she welcomed them, wanted to feel them more intimately.

Her jacket dropped to the ground and then he was unbuttoning the front fasteners of her dress.

Even as she was telling herself that this was a mistake her body was welcoming him, betraying her again, taking her over so that her mind was clouded and confused, divorced from all rational thought.

Jordan's hands found the lacy material of her bra and pushed it to one side, then his fingers connected with her naked breast, stroking and caressing her until she was incoherent with need, her body screaming for him.

His lips captured hers again in a drugging kiss then moved lower to her neck, his fingers caressing the tight, hard bud of her nipple.

'You see, you don't hate me at all, Charlotte,' he whispered as his mouth travelled upwards to find hers again. 'Shall we go somewhere more comfortable and finish this?' As he pulled back and looked deep into her eyes, all she could do was nod weakly.

She didn't want to feel like this, out of control and needy. All her life she'd been so independent. Letting Jordan affect her like this was risking getting hurt, especially as she knew how ruthless he was. But she couldn't help it. She just wasn't strong enough to pull back.

CHAPTER NINE

THE air was dry and hot in the boardroom and the meeting seemed to be stretching on forever.

Charlotte watched Jordan as he sat in the chair that not so long ago would have been occupied by her father. Strong and resolute, filled with enthusiasm and dynamic new ideas, he was easily generating a feeling of support and fervour in the people who sat around the long, polished table.

The essence of what he was saying at the moment was that he expected everyone to put his or her weight behind him.

Would anybody dare not to? Charlotte thought wryly. Her eyes drifted thoughtfully over him. He looked extremely attractive in the dark suit with a pristine white shirt and silver-grey tie, every inch the successful businessman. Jordan picked up a pen and played with it as he talked, and her eyes moved to his hand, watching him, and suddenly her mind was drifting away from the boardroom towards what had transpired between them in her bedroom last night.

Jordan's hands roaming over her body arousing her more and more, finding the warm core of her womanhood and tantalising her with promises of much more pleasurable delights.

When he entered her she had been gasping with need, her hands raking and scratching over his back, her eyes closed as she tried to concentrate on keeping the exquisite ecstasy alive for as long as possible.

'You're so gorgeous...' he had murmured huskily

against her ear, moving slowly at first, pacing himself and increasing her need for him to such a pitch that she hadn't thought it was possible to feel so much pleasure.

She remembered how she had cried out for him, and together they had capitulated to the wild, blissful feeling of complete satisfaction.

Then she remembered the feeling of shame afterwards as she'd lain cradled against him, her head resting on his chest. She had been ashamed of wanting him so much, of loving him so much, despite the fact that she knew what kind of man he was and that for him this was just sex.

Lying there in the afterglow of love, their bodies hot and tightly entwined, she had thought that she couldn't despise herself enough for this. Yet when he had reached to kiss her again she had kissed him back, and the wild need for him had risen inside her all over again.

She had pretended to be asleep when he had left her bed in the early hours of this morning. Had kept her eyes tightly closed as he moved around getting dressed and gathering his belongings.

He had reached to kiss her on the cheek and she had been filled with a bittersweet sadness, a longing for him to whisper just one word of love, even if he hadn't meant it, just one sweet word. But of course he hadn't and to have hoped for it was totally naïve. She wanted him to feel the same depth of feeling that burnt inside her, because she was in love with him, but the reality was he never would.

Jordan glanced down the table and their eyes met suddenly. The gleam in his eye made her feel flustered and self-conscious. It also brought an answering surge of adrenalin, as desire seemed to appear from nowhere.

'Right, well, that seems to be everything; we'll close the meeting and get on with the day's work,' Jordan said decisively.

Charlotte let her breath out in a shaky sigh as she gathered the papers in front of her and got up to follow everyone out of the room.

This power Jordan had over her emotions was truly scary, she thought. Just one look, one smile and she wanted him with a fierceness that was astounding. She was going to have to take great care at keeping her guard up around him, because if he guessed she was really in love with him it would be mortifying. She would lose the last vestige of her pride and he'd be terribly amused.

'Charlotte, if you have a minute, I'd like a word.' Jordan's firm tone halted her before she could escape with the rest of the staff.

She wanted to ignore him and keep walking but she knew it would serve no purpose. He'd just follow her into her office. And anyway it was best to play this cool, keep up outward appearances.

'Yes, Jordan?' She was delighted at how aloof she sounded, no hint of the turbulent emotion within.

'Sit down.' He pulled out the chair next to him, but she pretended she hadn't noticed and returned instead to the place she had been occupying previously at the other end of the table.

The door closed behind Jordan's secretary and they were left alone.

For a long moment Jordan said nothing, just watched her intently. Her hair was a mass of shiny curls that she had tied back from her face, her skin was pale and yet there was a blush along her cheeks that told him she was not as cool and controlled as she looked.

His eyes drifted lower towards the white blouse, where the lacy outline of her bra was just visible.

'What do you want?' She spoke abruptly, unable to bear the tension between them a moment longer. The way he was looking at her was making her senses reel.

He smiled calmly and walked down the length of the table to perch next to her against the shiny wood surface. 'How do you think the meeting went?'

'You're not seeking my approval, are you?' She couldn't restrain the sarcasm in her tone. 'Because after the way you've gained control here, you are never going to get it, Jordan.'

'I was simply seeking your opinion.' He reached out a hand and tipped her chin so that she was forced to look him in the eye. 'What's the matter with you? I thought we had overcome the problems between us last night.'

'Heavens, Jordan, it will take more than a pleasant roll in the sack to overcome my aversion for the way you've behaved regarding the business.' She jerked away from his hand. 'And please don't touch me—people can see every movement through these glass walls. We don't want to start tongues wagging.'

'Perish the thought,' Jordan said drily.

'Now, if that's all you wanted…' Charlotte scraped her chair back and stood up. 'I've got lots of work waiting for me in my office.'

He drummed his fingers impatiently against the polished table as the door closed behind her. Then watched her moving gracefully through the office with a feeling of complete and utter frustration.

Even though they had made love a number of times last night he still wanted her. Wanted her more than he could ever remember wanting a woman, wanted to tame that fire in her spirit, bring her under his control completely and yet…at the same time when she looked at him there was an expression of such vulnerability that he fiercely wanted to protect her, throw up his hands and tell her she could have anything she wanted, anything.

Charlotte sat back down at her desk. Had that just gone very badly? She wasn't sure at all. All she knew was that she needed to treat the emotions that flowed between them with the same casual ease Jordan did, and that didn't come easy to her. Maybe she had been a bit too cool, especially about last night. Pride was a difficult emotion to balance.

Frank came in and put the plans for the new apartments down on her desk. 'That meeting was interesting, wasn't it?' he said. 'Jordan is a very astute businessman.'

'Yes, he is.' Charlotte couldn't argue with that.

'We are all going to miss Simon, though,' Frank added softly. 'He's been the backbone of this company for as long as I can remember. And he's a good man.'

'Yes.' Charlotte looked up at him. 'Thanks, Frank.'

'What for? I'm only speaking the truth.' He smiled. 'I know this transition period can't be easy for you.'

'No, it's not.' Charlotte glanced over as Jordan left the boardroom, watched as he stopped to talk to one of the secretaries in the hallway. 'But in fairness I don't think it's an easy time for Jordan either,' she reflected softly. 'It will take a few months before we all settle down into the new way of things and in the meantime he will need all our help.' As she said the words, Charlotte realised she truly meant them. All right, she would never admit to Jordan's face that she would support him and work as part of the team wholeheartedly, because to do so felt like disloyalty to her father. But privately she had to grudgingly admit he was good for the company. And if she had to be really honest she knew her father's mind hadn't been centred wholly on work for a while now. In fact, if it hadn't been for him taking Jordan on as a partner, they might all be in a terrible mess.

The acknowledgement turned painfully in her mind. It was something she really didn't want to face up to.

'Well, he's the type of person who inspires confidence, isn't he? I think everyone is with him one hundred per cent.' Frank smiled.

'Yes...' Charlotte reached for the papers in front of her and tried to close everything out bar work.

'When does Jordan want those final figures for last month's sales?' she asked as Frank turned for the door.

'They aren't needed until tomorrow. But he said if you could have them on his desk this afternoon he'd be grateful.'

'OK. I'm seeing a rep in ten minutes and I still have to give my OK on these colour swatches, but I'll do it at lunch time.'

'Fair enough.'

Charlotte glanced across at Jordan's office. A man from the planning department was sitting opposite him now and they were deep in conversation. Jordan had taken off the jacket of his suit and rolled his shirtsleeves up, a sure sign that things were hotting up in there.

She reapplied her attention to the work in hand. The phone rang on her desk and she picked it up impatiently.

'Charlotte McCann here,' she said, balancing the phone under her chin so that she could continue to arrange the swatches on the cards in front of her.

'Charlotte, it's David. Please don't hang up.'

She was so surprised to hear his voice that she almost dropped the phone. 'David, this isn't a good time,' she said, putting down the swatches and pushing a few tendrils of her hair back from her face in agitation.

'I've been trying to get hold of you for days. Did you get any of the messages I left for you?'

He sounded cross, which irritated her, After all, he was the one in the wrong...he was the one who had behaved badly. 'Things are very busy, David, and I don't have time for this.'

'I just need a few minutes to speak to you.' His voice was suddenly pleading. 'For old times' sake, won't you at least give me that?'

Charlotte sighed. She had been meaning to phone him and end things on a civil note anyway, not that he really deserved it. But she realised now that their relationship had just run its course and would have died a natural death anyhow, even without her friend Linda's intervention.

As she hesitated David cut in. 'Look, this won't take long. I'm downstairs in the foyer.'

Charlotte's eyebrows rose in surprise. 'What, here in this building?'

'Yes,' he said quietly. 'And if you don't come down, I'll come up. Because I mean to see you today one way or another.'

Charlotte glanced nervously over towards Jordan; he was still deeply engrossed in conversation. She couldn't face David coming up here, making a scene. What the heck? she thought. She might as well go down and sort this out once and for all. 'OK, I'll be down in a minute.'

She smoothed her hair back and straightened the neck of her white blouse as she moved through to the hallway. Frank stuck his head up from his desk as he saw her walking towards the lifts.

'Where are you going?' he asked.

'I've a visitor in the foyer. I won't be long.'

As the lift descended to the ground floor Charlotte marvelled at how little the prospect of seeing David again mattered to her. But now that she thought about it he had never managed to raise her temperature…except when he'd told her about Linda.

The lift door opened and there he was. Charlotte had always thought David was quite a handsome guy, dark hair, very tall and well built. He was also artistically trendy—the pinstripe suit, mauve shirt and matching satin tie were testament to that. She had always thought he was a strong character too and yet now, as she looked at him, she noticed for the first time that there was an insipid quality about him. Maybe it was the way his dark hair flopped onto his forehead in a style that was slightly too long to suit him. Or maybe it was the smile, or the way his eyes couldn't quite meet hers.

He stepped towards her eagerly. For an awful moment she thought he was going to kiss her and she stepped back.

'Hello, David.'

'Hi. You look good.' His eyes slipped down over her in warm appreciation. 'I've missed you so much, Charlie.'

'I don't really have time for this—'

'Look, I know I hurt you—'

'And this really isn't the time or place,' Charlotte continued firmly.

'But you never seem to be at home these days, and there is so much we need to say to each other.'

Charlotte shook her head. 'We don't have anything to say to each other. Listen, David, I'm not angry…I know now that we were never suited. The glue that held us together as a couple was just our similar line of work.'

'Don't say that, Charlie—'

'But it's true.' Charlotte glanced at her watch. 'Anyway, I'll have to get back to work. No hard feelings, and I wish you well for the future, but please don't contact me again.'

As she made to turn away he caught hold of her wrist. 'I believe your father is retiring from the company.'

'How do you know that?' Charlotte was so surprised that she allowed herself to be drawn closer towards him. 'The staff were only told this morning.'

'You know what this business is like. There have been rumours for a while, so is it true?'

She nodded and then found herself pulled to one side of the foyer.

'Please, David, don't cause a scene,' she whispered, very conscious that they were now the subjects of scrutiny from the women on the reception desk.

'I've got something to ask you.' His voice became low and conspiratorial. 'And don't worry, it's just to do with business, nothing else. A marvellous opportunity has come up with a multinational firm. They have offered me a contract to redesign the interiors of all their hotels. It will mean I'll have to take on lots of new staff. It's the Sheldon group and you know they are worldwide.'

'I'm impressed, but why are you telling me?'

'Well, if your father has retired I thought that would leave the way clear for you to come in on the deal with me. We'd be a great team, and I'd make it well worth your while.'

Charlotte shook her head. 'We couldn't work together,' she said firmly. 'And anyway I'm happy here.'

'Did you ever get those shares that your father talked about?' He watched the colour flood into her face. 'No, I didn't think so.'

'I'll get some shares one day, but I've never been bothered about it, you know that.'

'Yes, I know.' David nodded. 'But I'm offering you a great deal…and mega money. And if you are worried about this getting personal, then don't. It's purely business. I accept that things are over between us. Please, just think about this.' He lowered his voice even more and leaned even closer. 'It's too good an opportunity to miss and I could really do with your talent.'

Before Charlotte could answer the lift doors opened and to her dismay Jordan strode out. He took in the situation at a glance and she saw his jaw hardening, his eyes narrowing. 'What the heck is going on here?' he demanded. 'I've been waiting for those figures, Charlotte—didn't Frank tell you I needed them straight away?'

She frowned. Frank hadn't told her any such thing. 'Those figures aren't due until tomorrow, but I said I'd have them on your desk this afternoon,' she answered calmly. 'I've been busy.'

'I can see that.' Jordan glanced over at David, who gave him a strained smile.

'Nice to see you again, Jordan,' he said brightly.

'I'd like to say the same, David, but these are business hours. Haven't you got any work to go to?'

'I'm on very important business actually.' David smiled. He looked over at Charlotte. 'So what about dinner this evening and we can talk properly about this?'

'Charlotte is busy this evening,' Jordan answered for her. 'Now, if you don't mind, we have got work to do even if you haven't.'

David looked for a moment as if he was going to put up an argument. But one glance at Jordan and he changed his mind. 'OK, I'm going. I'll ring you later, Charlotte.' With a weak smile in her direction David turned and headed through the revolving glass door out into the sunshine.

Charlotte glanced up at Jordan, her eyes shimmering with fury. How dared he answer for her, how dared he march down here as if he owned her? Conscious of how avidly the receptionists were watching, she turned and walked back into the lift with Jordan following. But as soon as the doors had snapped closed her cool vanished. 'What the hell do you think you are playing at, marching down here and ordering me around, and in front of David of all people?' She angled her chin up defiantly and met his eyes. 'You are not my keeper, Jordan.'

'No, but I'm your boss.'

Something about the way he said that made Charlotte flinch.

'What did he want anyway?' Jordan asked coolly.

'He wanted to talk to me over dinner tonight and you had no right to answer for me like that.'

'Oh, come on, you didn't really want to go out with him, did you?' Jordan reached over and to her disquiet pressed the button on the lift, stopping them between floors.

'I think that is my business, not yours.'

'The guy is bad news, Charlie. He's the creep who slept with your best friend, for heaven's sake.'

'She wasn't my best friend,' Charlotte reminded him edgily.

Jordan shrugged. 'I thought you'd be pleased that I came down and got rid of him for you.'

'Well, I'm not pleased.'

'There's an old saying that goes "once bitten, twice shy"; maybe you should reflect on that.'

The arrogant statement fuelled her temper even more.

'Just because we have slept together, Jordan, it doesn't give you the right to tell me what to do in my love life. And for your information the main reason David came around here was to offer me a job, a damn good one at that, working for the Sheldon group, redesigning the interiors of their hotels…worldwide.'

Jordan's eyes narrowed on her face. 'I don't care if he has offered you work redesigning hotels for the entire galaxy. We have an agreement, Charlie. You are committed to staying here, working for me for one year.' His voice hardened. 'Or are you reneging on our deal?'

'I'm not reneging on anything,' she said quickly, the tone of his voice making her instantly regret telling him anything about David's offer.

'So you've told David you don't want the job?'

'Yes…yes, I've told him,' she admitted angrily.

'Good.' For a second Jordan's eyes moved to her lips. 'Because I don't want you seeing David again…in any capacity whatsoever.' The husky admission made her heart miss a beat painfully.

'I want you exclusively, Charlotte.' Then he put his hand on the wall next to her and bent to kiss her. She tried to make herself turn her head away, but it was the same old problem—as soon as Jordan got within a few inches of her she couldn't find the strength to move.

His lips were deliciously seductive and the hand that held her face was tenderly gentle. She felt her emotions swirl and mist with confusion. And then she was kissing him back.

He smiled as he pulled away, his eyes lazily taking in her flushed countenance and the softness of her lips. 'I don't want David coming around here to see you again. Do I make myself clear?' The words were laced with an undertone completely at odds with the words. 'And you will be having dinner with me tonight.'

The arrogance of that request struck the rawness inside Charlotte, stirring it viciously. 'Oh, I see…you mean I should make myself available for you…as per our agreement.' Her voice trembled alarmingly.

She was gratified by the dark look of anger in Jordan's eyes. But the feeling of triumph was short-lived.

'Yes, that's exactly what I mean,' Jordan said coolly.

He pulled away from her and pushed the lift button so that it started to glide smoothly on to the top floor.

'After dinner we will be attending a drinks party. It's an important business occasion, there'll be a lot of our associates present and it will be a good opportunity for us to network with them.'

She might have known that when he had stated he wanted her, he had been talking in the business sense. How stupid—for the tiniest fraction of a second she had hoped he was jealous and annoyed simply because he wanted her, not because of business.

'I'll pick you up at seven-thirty.' The steely look in his

eye and the reminder of his ruthless hold over her made her seethe inside, but she held herself ramrod straight and kept her dignity.

'Fine, I'll be ready.'

CHAPTER TEN

CHARLOTTE was sitting at her dressing table putting the finishing touches to her make-up. She looked a bit pale, she thought, reaching to put a brighter lipstick on. But then she hadn't been feeling well for a few days now.

It was seven weeks since Jordan had taken over the company. Seven dizzying weeks of hard work in the office followed by numerous PR engagements in the evening, each designed to boost the profile of the company.

Charlotte had to admit she had enjoyed the challenges, and she had very much enjoyed being by Jordan's side. Not that she would ever have admitted it to him, of course.

The first night she had accompanied him to dinner and a drinks party she had felt awkwardly unsure of exactly what he expected of her. Their argument earlier that day had simmered beneath the surface of their conversation but as the evening wore on she had found herself forgetting all about it. And Jordan had been a perfect gentleman—in fact maybe too much of a gentleman, because when he had brought her home he had kissed her only once, briefly, and then left her aching for so much more.

That first outing had set the precedent. Each time they had gone out it had been pleasant, but he had made no attempt to move on her sexually.

Of course they had been on business-related trips, and he did have a lot on at the moment. Things were manic at the office; she had never known it so busy. But even as she was telling herself these things she knew she was making excuses. If Jordan had wanted to stay and make love to her when he'd brought her home, he could have. He knew how he affected her, knew she was his for the taking.

Anyway, she should be delighted that he was backing off. He spelled danger; he was callous and calculating. She was better off without him. The words echoed hollowly inside her.

The problem was that, no matter how many times she told herself those things, the words still seemed to fade to cardboard as soon as she saw him. She still wanted him, still loved him. There was something about Jordan that fired her blood, excited her and turned her on in a way she had never been turned on before.

He was bringing her to a promotional party to celebrate the completion of the Richmond apartments this evening. It promised to be an impressive affair, as they were holding it at one of London's hottest nightclubs and various people in the advertising and media world would be attending. Maybe, when tonight was over, Jordan would be feeling a little more relaxed, and when he brought her home this evening he would make a move on her.

Or maybe she should make a move on him?

She stared at her reflection in the mirror. Inviting Jordan to make love to her would be a huge climb-down and she didn't know if her pride would allow it. Even if she did want him so much that it hurt.

If only Jordan hadn't got control of the company by blackmailing her father…if only she could forget what kind of man he really was. He was so lovely in so many other ways, charming, funny, clever, sexy…

But the fact remained that she did know the truth, so it was either accept him for what he was or put him out of her mind forever.

The doorbell rang and she glanced at her watch. That would be Jordan; he was always punctual. Taking a deep breath, she went to let him in.

'Hi.' He smiled at her as the door swung open and his eyes slipped approvingly down over her figure in the blue silk dress, making apprehension and longing twist together inside her in a powerful play on her emotions. 'You look lovely.'

'Thank you.' She smiled back at him. He looked good as well. The suit he wore was well cut and a deep midnight-blue, and beneath it he wore a lighter blue shirt and matching tie. The colours seemed to emphasise the darkness of his hair, giving him an almost Mediterranean look.

Forgetting about Jordan Lynch would be no easy task, she thought unhappily. In fact, she didn't think she would ever be able to get him out of her system.

'Would you like to come in for a drink before we leave?' she asked politely.

'No, better not.' Jordan glanced at his watch. 'I think we should go.'

'Of course.' She reached to get her wrap and her purse and followed him outside onto the street.

'So everything is in place for tonight,' she said brightly as he unlocked the car and she slipped into the passenger side. 'Everyone coming who should be coming?'

'I think so. We've had a pretty good response from our advertisers and we should get a few photos and mentions in some of the top property magazines.' Jordan pulled the car out smoothly into the traffic. 'Tomorrow will be the real test though when the show apartments open for public viewing. Tonight is more about generating a high profile, and entertaining the staff into the bargain.'

'Yes, everyone is thrilled that the venue is The Tank.'

'It's a pretty good club. Have you been?' He took his attention off the road for a moment.

'No,' she smiled. 'I have to admit I haven't been to a club in ages.'

Charlotte looked out at the sunny evening. The trees in

the avenue were cloaked with the heavy fullness of their summer greenery, and flowers tumbled in profusion from window boxes and hanging baskets. People were strolling towards the park in short-sleeved T-shirts and summer dresses. 'I'm probably getting old and boring, but to be honest I'd be just as happy with a drive out to a country pub on an evening like this as with a visit to the top club.' She shrugged and grinned. 'That's very sad, isn't it?'

Jordan looked over at her and laughed. 'Not really. I was thinking the same thing earlier. And if tonight wasn't solely for work, I'd steal you away immediately.'

Charlotte liked the sound of that. 'Maybe we can do that another day,' she suggested lightly.

'Day after tomorrow?' Jordan looked over at her and then smiled when she didn't answer him immediately. 'Sunday…it's your niece's christening. You haven't forgotten, have you?'

'No, of course not.' She shook her head. She hadn't forgotten the christening but she had been hoping he might ask her out tomorrow night. Everything workwise would be completed, well for the time being at any rate, and it would be a Saturday night. It would have been nice to go out with him on a Saturday just for the hell of it—no work excuses, no family excuses for them to be together, just them on their own.

'I believe they've booked a room at a very picturesque coaching house for the party afterwards.'

'Yes.' Charlotte looked across at Jordan. 'You've been talking to Steve recently, I take it?'

'We played golf last Sunday.'

Charlotte glanced down at her hands. Would her family life always be so intertwined with him? she wondered, and suddenly she had a vision of arriving at Jennifer's at some point in the future and finding Jordan there with a girlfriend.

The thought was so horrifying that she felt it slam into her like a fist. Hurriedly she put the image away.

'Steve said your father is doing very well in France, that his health is much improved,' Jordan said as he swung the car into a parking space next to the wine bar where they had arranged to meet some of their co-workers from the office before going on to the party.

'Yes, he's not doing badly at all.' Charlotte smiled. 'He hates to admit it but I think he really is enjoying retirement.'

'Now I know where you get that stubborn streak from.' Jordan smiled back at her.

'You think I'm stubborn?'

Jordan's grin stretched wider. 'Only the most stubborn woman I've ever met. But then your birthday is in August, isn't it, which makes you a Leo? Very obstinate star sign.'

'What rubbish. You've just made that up.' She grinned at him. 'How do you know that my birthday is in August anyway?'

'I looked up your file at work, soon after I joined the company. Found out a few things about you.' He gave her a teasing look. 'First law of the jungle, find out all there is to know about your adversaries, so you can keep one step ahead.'

'So that's where I've been going wrong!' She laughed. 'Obviously I should have pulled your file months ago.'

He nodded. 'Big mistake.'

'So if I had pulled your file, what would it have told me?'

'Let's see: Capricorn, ambitious, tenacious—'

'Ah, but I already know all that. Would it have told me any of your weaknesses?'

'I think you need a private consultation to find that out.' Jordan smiled.

For a moment there was a warmth between them that

sent shivers of awareness racing through her. Then Jordan turned away. 'I suppose we should go in; we don't want to keep everyone waiting.'

Although Charlotte agreed and also turned to get out of the car she couldn't help wishing that they weren't meeting other people tonight. She just wanted to be alone with Jordan. And suddenly she didn't even care if she was playing with fire or not.

The wine bar was doing a brisk trade and at first Charlotte couldn't see any of the people from the office. Then she spotted a few of them behind a pillar.

'Over here,' Frank called. 'And you're late. We were almost off to the club without you.'

'It won't even be open yet,' Charlotte said with a grin.

'Ten-thirty is the time the party is due to kick off,' Jordan said from behind her. 'So can I get anyone a drink?'

As Jordan headed for the bar with the drinks order, Charlotte chatted with Frank's wife, Donna, an attractive woman in her late twenties. 'I can't believe we are going to The Tank for this party,' she said in excitement. 'I've wanted to go there for ages but it's really hard to get in. They say it's *the* place to be seen. Apparently the décor is fantastic; you go down in a lift to the basement and the walls surrounding you are full of tropical fish.'

'Well, I'm looking forward to having a peek at the décor.' Charlotte laughed.

'For heaven's sake, Charlie, you are under strict instructions to switch off from work. No measuring up the windows,' Frank laughed. 'We've done enough of that all day at the office.'

Jordan brought back the drinks and Charlotte reached to take her glass of white wine. As she raised the glass to her lips the smell of the alcohol made her stomach suddenly churn and she couldn't drink it.

'You OK?' Jordan looked across the table at her.

She nodded and smiled and was glad that the conversation carried on around them in a light-hearted way because she didn't want to create a fuss. But in reality she wasn't feeling at all well. She felt a bit dizzy and the nauseous feeling that had struck persisted.

As the men launched into a deep conversation about cricket, Charlotte glanced over at Frank's wife and saw that she was also drinking white wine.

'Is your wine all right, Donna?' she asked the other woman quietly.

'Fine. Why?'

'Mine seems a bit overpowering.'

She watched as the other woman picked up her glass and sniffed at it then took a sip. 'It's fine,' she pronounced, then looked at Charlotte in concern. 'You don't look very well.'

'I'll be fine in a minute.'

Even so, for the rest of the time in the bar Charlotte sat very still, hoping the feeling would pass and not get worse. And she couldn't bring herself to touch the glass of wine again.

Frank swigged back the rest of his beer. 'Hurry up, Charlotte, we should be moving on to the club in a few minutes. Jordan wants us to be there before the photographers arrive.'

'I'm ready when you are,' Charlotte said, hastily moving the glass further away.

'Are you sure you are OK?' Jordan asked her quietly once they had stepped back outside into the air. 'You looked very pale in there.'

'Too many late nights recently.' Charlotte smiled.

'It has been pretty hectic. You've either been working late every night or you've been out with me.'

'At least it's the weekend and we can relax tomorrow and unwind.'

'Well, I'll have to go down to the apartments in the morning as it's the first opening,' he said lightly. 'But you should take it easy.'

They only had to walk around the corner to the club and it was a beautiful evening. Everyone was laughing and joking and Charlotte joined in, trying not to think about the fact that she had felt a bit nauseous this morning as well, and yesterday at lunch time the smell of coffee had really set her on edge.

It was nothing, she told herself briskly. A bit of sensitivity…or perhaps she really was overtired.

A little while later they were amongst a heaving throng of people in a club that was like being in an aquarium, sharks and tropical fish circling around the glass walls in a neon glow of colour. The lighting was incredible: pillars of illumination lit the room, leaving the dance floor and most of the seating in a blue half-light as if they were in a tank under the sea.

As Jordan was caught up with members of the Press Charlotte excused herself and went into the bathroom to check her make-up.

As she walked over to the vanity basins and saw her reflection she got a bit of a shock. Her skin was deathly white and her eyes seemed to dominate her small, delicate face.

'Are you feeling any better?' Donna came and stood beside her and immediately Charlotte busied herself finding a lipstick in her bag.

'Yes, I'm fine; it seems silly really but it was just the smell of the wine.' Charlotte applied more lipstick and gave a sweep of blusher over her cheeks, determined not to give in to the feeling of weakness inside.

'That reminds me of when I was pregnant with Josh.' Donna leaned forward to put on some mascara. 'But with me it was the smell of tea—hell, that was awful. I was sick for weeks.'

Charlotte was glad she had left her hair loose tonight; at least it hid her face a little. Fluffing it up, she tried to pretend that she was concentrating on her looks, not suddenly homing in on the possibility that she could be pregnant.

She was late, now she thought of it, but that could just be stress after the worry of her father and everything. Couldn't it? Charlotte felt a sharp pang of complete panic for a moment.

Luckily Donna was the talkative type and she carried on, blithely unaware that Charlotte was hardly listening. 'I remember a New Year's Eve party as well; I spent nearly the whole night in the bathroom. But that was food poisoning…'

She wasn't pregnant, Charlotte told herself firmly. OK, she was, what, two weeks late at the most? Or was it more? When *had* she last…?

Aware that Donna had said something that required an answer, Charlotte hastily pulled herself together. 'I think I've just got a bug but it's a bit of bad timing to be feeling under the weather.' She smiled. 'What with all these photographers waiting to snap our pictures for the publicity shots.'

'Yes…' Donna agreed. 'I had my hair done at a top salon especially for the occasion.'

'I'll have to hide at the back.' Charlotte grinned as they turned to head outside. 'It's as good an excuse as any—I hate having my photograph taken.'

They stood at the bar for a while and Charlotte started to feel a bit better as she sipped a mineral water. She wasn't pregnant, she told herself firmly.

'Who is that woman?' she asked Frank as she saw an attractive brunette talking to Jordan across the room.

'That's Benita.' It was Jordan's secretary, Laura, who answered the question. 'You know, the model.'

'You mean Jordan's ex-girlfriend?' Charlotte did a double take on the other woman. Now that she looked at her she could see it was Benita. She looked stunning in a long white dress that curved with her slender body and glowed under the neon lights.

'I don't think she likes to class herself as an ex.' Laura laughed. 'She's never off the phone to him.'

Charlotte was very taken aback by that news. 'They are still good friends, then?'

'Oh, yes, very much so. But then you know what Jordan is like—a real charmer.' Laura grinned. 'She agreed to come tonight for some promotional photos to boost the level of interest in the occasion and apparently she's going to do the same at the apartments tomorrow. If you ask me, there might be a reconciliation on the cards.'

Charlotte sipped at her mineral water and tried to tell herself she didn't care, but she was lying, because when she turned around and saw the two of them posing for a photographer, Jordan's arm resting around Benita's waist, she felt a stab of jealousy unlike anything she had ever known.

The music was cranked up even louder and Laura and her husband left them to go out onto the dance floor.

'It's a great place, isn't it?' Frank said. 'I bet those glass tanks around the walls cost a fortune.'

'Yes, I bet they did.' But the truth was that Charlotte was hardly listening now. She shot a glance over at Benita again. There was still a crowd of people around her, but she couldn't see Jordan now.

'Hello, Charlie.' A man tapped Charlotte on the shoulder and, turning, she was surprised to find herself face to face with David.

'What are you doing here?' she asked in surprise.

'I thought everyone in the know would be here tonight.' He grinned. 'After all the publicity and hype about this launch party I didn't want to miss it.' His eyes swept down over her figure. 'You look great, by the way.'

'Thanks.' Charlotte felt a bit embarrassed by the compliment.

'When I didn't hear anything from you I took it you weren't interested in my job offer,' David said smoothly.

'I'm pretty settled where I am.'

'Shame.' David looked disappointed. 'Well, you know where I am if you ever change your mind.'

'Yes...'

'I'd better get back; I'm on a date.' David looked over his shoulder towards one of the tables. 'But I don't think it's going to last very long; she's not really my type.'

'No one I know, then?' Charlotte grinned.

'No...no one you know.' He smiled at her sadly and then reached to kiss her on the cheek. 'See you around, Charlie.'

'Yes, see you around.'

As Charlotte turned back to the bar she was surprised to find Jordan standing behind her. He smiled at her, a tinge of irony in his dark eyes. 'At least he succeeded in bringing some colour to your cheeks.'

'He was just being polite. He's here with a date actually.'

'Yes, I saw her earlier, a pretty brunette.'

'And you've got a good eye for a brunette, haven't you, Jordan?' Charlotte couldn't resist the quip.

'I'm more into blondes these days.' The quiet remark and the way he was looking at her made Charlotte's temperature increase dramatically.

He really was a smooth talker, she thought wryly. She shouldn't fall for it, should have more sense. Yet as he put a hand at her back, the touch of his skin against hers made feelings of desire instantly surface.

'Come on, let's go and have a few photographs taken together.'

'What's the matter, has Benita had to rush off to another venue?' she asked slightly breathlessly as he steered her over to where he had been standing earlier.

'I think she has.' Jordan smiled at her. 'But not to worry, she'll be back to pose decoratively around the apartments tomorrow.'

'Quite a coup getting your ex to give her time like that.'

'I can be very persuasive when I need to be.'

'Don't I know it?' Charlotte said drily.

She was glad that the photographers joined them at that moment, curtailing that particular line of conversation.

For a while they were under the scrutiny of several different cameras, but as soon as possible Charlotte escaped from the limelight, content to watch from the sidelines as more of the office staff joined in.

'Going well, isn't it?' Frank said happily as he came to stand beside her.

'Yes, I'm sure Jordan is pleased.'

'Especially as Benita came. Everywhere she goes she's followed by the paparazzi. So we'll be in a few more newspapers tomorrow.'

'Yes…very fortunate.' Charlotte tried to keep her voice light. 'Where has she gone now, do you know?'

'She's opening a new club somewhere else tonight. Apparently she only popped in here between gigs as a special favour.'

'Lucky Jordan.'

'Yes, lucky Jordan indeed,' Frank drawled. 'Apparently he's taking her out for dinner tomorrow night as well.'

'How do you know that?' Charlotte frowned.

'I was standing next to her when she reminded him of their date. Seven o'clock at La Fortuna.'

Charlotte felt her heart starting to speed up painfully against her chest. So now she knew why Jordan hadn't asked her out tomorrow night. And very possibly why he hadn't been interested in making love to her for so long.

'Maybe Laura is right and they are getting back together again. Fancy that.' It was a tremendous effort to sound so relaxed. 'Our boss is a real dark horse, isn't he?'

'You could say that,' Frank laughed.

Charlotte followed his gaze back towards Jordan, who was now talking to a very attractive female photographer.

Who was she kidding? Charlotte thought angrily. Jordan was no dark horse: he changed his girlfriends with the weather and he had never bothered to deny it.

The stark fact hit her with brutal clarity.

'You know, Frank, I think I'll make tracks for home now.'

'Really? Well, if you hang on Donna and I will give you a lift; we have to be back for the babysitter anyway.'

'No, it's out of your way and I'm fine taking a taxi.' Charlotte glanced back over towards Jordan. 'Will you make my excuses to Jordan for me?'

'Sure.' Frank nodded.

If there was an award going for best acting performance tonight, I should receive it, Charlotte thought as she left the club and climbed into a taxi outside.

And to think it had actually crossed her mind that she should seduce Jordan this evening… Really, she had lost her senses where that man was concerned.

But then, she had always known deep down that this was how an involvement with Jordan would end. If he wasn't seeing Benita it would just be someone else. Jordan didn't believe in long-term relationships, or love. He had told her that very clearly.

So what would she do if she was pregnant?

The question crept in, taking her unawares. And suddenly her mind was flicking forward along a path of vivid imaginings. She saw herself pregnant and forced to work for him, knowing he didn't want her, knowing he didn't love her, and it was an unbearable picture.

As panic mounted inside her she tried to damp it down. She didn't know for sure and it could just be stress. First thing tomorrow she would buy one of those testing kits.

The taxi pulled up outside her flat and she hurried out. As she took her front-door key out of her handbag the sound of a car door slamming and footsteps behind her made her look around nervously.

'Jordan! What are you doing here?'

He glared at her angrily. 'Call me old-fashioned, Charlie, but when I take a woman out for the evening I generally expect to drop her home as well.'

'Well, you were busy and I didn't like to drag you away from the party. I asked Frank to explain.' She felt suddenly breathless as he came closer. She didn't want him to touch her or come anywhere near her because she didn't know how she would react. Her emotions were all over the place.

'Well, Frank didn't explain very much. What's the matter? Are you feeling ill?'

Charlotte opened her mouth to tell him she was fine and then changed her mind. She didn't feel fine at all, she felt terrible. 'Yes, I do feel ill,' she admitted shakily. 'But I'll be OK after a good night's rest. I'm sorry you've left your party because of me and thanks for your concern but you should really go back there now—'

'Don't be ridiculous. I'm not going back to the party. I have no interest in going back.' He took the key from her hand and put it in the lock. 'The media circus is pretty much wrapped up there anyway. I'm coming inside with you.'

'Jordan, this isn't a good idea and I really...' Her protests were overruled as he opened the door and steered her firmly inside.

'So what do you think is wrong with you?' he asked, snapping on the light, his eyes raking over her in a close scrutiny that made her cringe.

'I...I don't know. I'm just not feeling well, that's all...' His forceful manner was really starting to unnerve her. She pulled away from him and put her wrap and her bag down on the hall table. 'I think if you just go I'll be OK in the morning.'

'Shall I make you a cup of tea?' He looked at her with a raised eyebrow. 'How about some chicken soup?' The teasing offer made her suddenly want to cry. She didn't want him to be nice to her; it just made it harder to keep away from him.

'I don't need chicken soup or looking after. I'm fine on my own, but thank you anyway.'

'Are you sure?' He stepped closer and raised her chin so that he could look at her again, but this time his manner had lost that bossy edge and seemed filled only with concern. That and the touch of his hands against her skin made the tears rise. Fiercely she blinked them away.

'Look, you don't need to pretend to be a nice guy around me. I know the truth...I know the real Jordan Lynch.'

'Do you?' He stroked the side of her face with one finger and the gentle touch fired her blood even more.

Suddenly she was remembering what had happened the last time they had stood so closely together in this hallway. And she couldn't let that happen again. As much as she wanted him, as much as all her senses cried out to just melt into his arms, she knew that it was a mistake and that she had to break away.

'Jordan, this situation is killing me, can't you see?' Her

voice broke on a sob and she pulled fiercely away from him. 'I can't go on like this, pretending everything is fine, having to work with you day in and day out, feeling the way I do… I can't be tied to you like this, I just can't!'

Jordan took a step back from her and watched her silently for a moment. Noted the ashen colour of her skin and the tears that spilled silently from her eyes.

For a long moment she thought he wasn't going to answer her. Then he shrugged.

'I'll have to think about the situation,' he said calmly.

'You mean you might be prepared to release me from our agreement?' She brushed the tears away, her heart slamming against her chest as she asked the question.

'I said I'd think about it.'

Then he turned and walked out of the apartment, closing the door quietly behind him.

CHAPTER ELEVEN

ESCAPING to Jennifer's house the next morning seemed a good idea on Saturday. She couldn't stand being in her empty flat, and having time on her hands to think definitely wasn't helping. So when her sister rang and asked if she wouldn't mind arriving early for the christening in order to give her a hand with the children, Charlotte jumped in with both feet and told her she'd come straight away and stay overnight.

However, if she had hoped the change of scene would help put Jordan out of her mind, she had reckoned without Jennifer. Because from the moment she arrived her sister asked ceaseless questions about how their relationship was progressing. Questions Charlotte wasn't ready to answer. And her prevarications only invited more questions.

Add to that a violent bout of sickness on Saturday evening and Charlotte started to wish she'd just stayed at home.

But somehow she got through it without having to tell Jen anything. In fact she coped magnificently. Helping to bathe the children this morning, she was laughing and joking with Harriet and even surprised herself at how well she was hiding her unhappiness.

But now, as the time approached for Jordan to arrive, she found herself wishing after all that she had opened up to her sister. She needed to talk to someone, she was confused and upset...and more scared than she had ever been in her life.

It was strange how you could still feel lonely in a house full of people, she thought as she put the finishing touches to her make-up and then stood back to inspect her reflection in the full-length mirror. Her hair was in a soft chignon, a few curling tendrils around her face.

She had lost weight, she noticed suddenly; the pale pink dress that had fitted her so well a few weeks ago now hung loosely on her slender frame. Probably due to the amount of times she had been sick over the last few days. But considering she felt so wretched she looked remarkably well; in fact her skin was glowing.

She heard a car pulling up outside and went to the bedroom window. It was Jordan, and Charlotte's heart started to bounce unsteadily just at the sight of his car. She watched as he stepped out into the sunshine. He looked handsome in a dark suit and a blue shirt and tie, and her heart seemed to twist inside her even more.

There was a part of her that wanted to run down the stairs and throw herself into his arms with the same lack of inhibition as Harriet. But of course she could never do that. She gave herself one final nervous check in the mirror. She would act as if she hadn't a care in the world, as if everything between them was fine, she reminded herself firmly. For one thing she had her pride and for another she couldn't let a whisper of any unpleasantness spoil the christening. Taking a deep breath, she went downstairs to let him in.

Harriet had beaten her to it and was outside on the driveway already, dancing around him in dizzying circles. Then she skipped in past Charlotte. 'Uncle Jordan is here,' she called like the town crier.

Jordan gave an amused smile, but she noticed when his eyes moved towards her how his expression cooled.

'Steve told you I was here last night, didn't he?' she checked. She had got Steve to ring him early this morning in case he had planned to pick her up on the way out here.

'Oh, yes, I got your message,' he said.

'Good. I wasn't sure if you had planned to give me a lift out here and I didn't want you to have a wasted journey.'

Did she sound as nervous as she felt? she wondered.

He didn't say anything to that, but his eyes took in everything about her appearance in one comprehensive sweep as he stepped into the hall.

'You look good,' he murmured.

For a brief moment he seemed too close to her and just the familiar pleasant scent of his aftershave brought a bittersweet surge of emotion inside her.

She stepped back and forced herself to smile politely. 'Thank you.' There was a moment of awkward silence and she was very grateful when Steven stepped out from the lounge and the two men shook hands. After that it seemed everything happened at once as her father and Ruth arrived in a taxi and Jennifer came downstairs with the baby, resplendent in a white christening robe.

Charlotte was glad to see that her father looked very well. He had acquired a healthy tan and the gaunt lines of worry from his face seemed to have faded. Ruth was also more relaxed than Charlotte could ever remember and she looked very attractive in a pale lemon suit with a wide-brimmed hat.

It was a happy family reunion and if things had been different between herself and Jordan it would have been absolutely perfect.

'I hate to break up the frivolity but I think it's time we went to the church,' Steve said, glancing at the clock on the mantelpiece. 'Jordan, will you take Simon and Ruth in your car with Charlotte?'

'Certainly,' Jordan agreed easily.

Charlotte felt relieved that she wasn't going to be left

alone with Jordan. Now, if she could just get through today without feeling sick, she would be eternally grateful, she thought.

There was a hushed silence as they all stood around the font. Charlotte held the baby in her arms, with Jordan by her side, as they each gave their solemn promise to watch over the child.

Then the vicar took the baby from her.

'I name this child Nicole Estelle,' he said.

As the cool water ran over the baby's forehead she gave a little whimper of protest but she didn't cry.

Charlotte's eyes met with Jordan's and they both smiled. If only things were different, she thought sadly, and felt a huge wave of emotion rise up inside her.

Knowing Jordan, she felt sure he would honour that pledge for his goddaughter. She knew he wasn't the type of man to make promises lightly. And he was so good around children…

Trying not to think too deeply about that, she concentrated instead on taking hold of Harriet's hand as she fidgeted beside her mother.

The service was short and then they headed out of the old church with its colourful stained-glass windows into the full force of the summer sunshine.

'That went well, didn't it?' Jordan smiled at her as they lined up outside for a few photographs. 'And I like the name they chose for the baby. Nicole is very pretty.'

'Let's have a picture just with the godparents now,' Steve said, coming over and placing Nicole in Charlotte's arms. Jordan placed an arm around her and pulled her close as they smiled for the photographer.

Steve's mother, a large lady in a pink outfit, waved over at Charlotte. 'You look good with a baby in your arms, Charlotte. Better get a move-on, now.'

Charlotte managed a weak smile in return. She really could have done without that remark.

What would Jordan say if she told him she was pregnant? The question burnt inside her.

She didn't dare look at him and couldn't wait to pull away from him once the photo was taken.

'Right, see everyone back at the hotel,' Steve said as he took Nicole from her arms. 'Your father and Ruth are coming back with us, by the way, Charlie.'

Charlotte felt an immediate burst of consternation. She didn't want to be left alone with Jordan, not now; she wasn't feeling emotionally strong enough for any kind of contact with him.

But she couldn't protest because it would have looked odd, so she swallowed down her misgivings and forced herself to go along with the arrangements. She was being ridiculous anyway, she told herself sternly. It was only a short drive to the hotel; surely she could get through fifteen minutes on her own with Jordan.

The sensible words soothed her until she was sitting next to him in his car and then one glance across at him and she wasn't too sure if she could get through five minutes, never mind fifteen. There were so many emotions racing around inside her.

What would he say if she suddenly blurted out the truth? she wondered. She imagined it in her mind, her voice clear and steady: I'm pregnant, Jordan. I did a test yesterday and it was positive.

She glanced over at him. He looked stern and withdrawn. How could she possibly tell him that? She knew very well he didn't want any serious involvements in his life and you could hardly get a more serious commitment than having a baby.

Hurriedly she glanced away again. The thing was, she really wanted this baby. She would be thirty-three in a few weeks. She wasn't getting any younger and she had always wanted a family. The question was, could she cope on her own…?

And what if Jordan didn't release her from their agreement? As the months passed he was going to know she was pregnant whether she told him or not.

'You're very quiet.' Jordan's voice made her nerves jump.

'Am I?' She gave him a weak smile. 'Sorry, I was miles away. How did things go at the apartments yesterday? Did many people turn up?' With extreme difficulty she steered the conversation away from anything emotive. They still had a party to get through and deeper topics could wait.

'Yes, there was a lot of interest and a few of the apartments have buyers lined up already.'

'That's good.'

'Yes, I'm quite satisfied,' he said. 'We can go on to the second phase of the development now with confidence.'

The words caused a tremor of unease inside her. 'Jordan, I meant it when I asked if you would release me from our agreement.' She spoke very quietly, but her eyes were filled with earnest appeal. 'I know we had an agreement and I really am sorry.'

'Sorry doesn't cut it, Charlotte,' he answered coldly as he turned the car up a narrow country lane leading to the old black and white Tudor coaching house. 'You gave me your word.'

'I know.' Her eyes shimmered emphatically now. 'But you don't really need me at the business—you could function perfectly well without me. There are plenty of good designers out there.'

'Maybe so, but now isn't a good time to be changing the head of the department.' Jordan pulled into the car park and found a space by the front entrance. 'Maybe in another six months we'll talk.'

'Six months!' Charlotte climbed out into the sunshine and stared at him in complete frustration. 'Please, Jordan...please reconsider.'

'We'll talk about this later,' he said with cool dismissal. 'I've got a christening party to attend and I don't want to stand out here arguing about something that has already been settled. I thought you were a woman of your word.'

'I am!' She walked hurriedly after him.

'You could have fooled me.'

The derisive words tore into her. But she could see where he was coming from—she *had* promised. Only things had changed; she was pregnant. How could she stay working for him now?

'I suppose this has something to do with that job David offered you?' he muttered as they walked through the red-carpeted foyer.

'No! As a matter of fact, it hasn't.'

Jordan sent her a look of complete disbelief. 'I'm not a complete idiot, Charlotte. But I must say, I thought after the way he behaved you'd have had more sense than to want to work for him. It just goes to show how women can be totally irrational.'

'Well, that's a sexist remark if ever I heard one. You're not exactly the most judicious person in the world when it comes to the opposite sex.'

'Where you're concerned, maybe,' he conceded drily. He flicked a glance over at her and watched the colour flare under her skin with a kind of lazy complacency. 'I have been more than understanding about some of your family problems.'

'My family problems have suited your purposes very well, Jordan,' she reminded him and then lowered her voice to a furious whisper as they passed some other people. 'You wanted control of the company and you got it.'

'Yes, I did.' He shrugged.

'And a viper would be more understanding. You treated my father appallingly—'

'The fact remains that we had a deal, Charlie,' he cut across her firmly. 'And I'm not in the mood to compromise.'

She would have made some kind of rejoinder to that except for the fact that they had reached the entrance to the wood-panelled dining room where the christening party was in full swing.

A waiter standing inside the doorway offered a glass of champagne to them, and then they made their way across to join her father and Ruth, who were standing next to the buffet table.

Simon beamed happily at them both. 'Tell me, how are things in the business, Jordan?' he asked. 'We haven't had time to talk about it.'

'Everything is just fine,' Jordan answered. 'The Richmond show apartments opened yesterday.'

'I must go over and have a look. We're here for a few days so I thought I might pop into the office to say hello to everyone as well.'

'They'd all like that,' Jordan said easily.

Despite the cheerful conversation around them, Jordan's eyes were dark and serious as they met with Charlotte's a few minutes later.

'I wonder how your father will feel if he knows you want to leave the business?' he enquired in a low undertone.

'He will understand,' she muttered angrily. 'And don't try to pretend you give a damn about how my father might feel.'

She walked away from him to talk to Steve's mother and then carefully avoided him for the next hour or so.

'Everything OK with you and Jordan?' Jennifer asked

once she had mingled with most of her guests around the room.

Charlotte nodded and changed the subject. 'I enjoyed the service; it was really lovely…brought a lump to my throat.'

'Yes, everyone said that.' Jennifer looked proudly down at her baby. 'Nicole was so good; she always is. So what's with you and Jordan?'

The swift change back to Jordan took her by surprise. 'We are not getting on very well,' she admitted.

Her sister laughed. 'Sparks fly whenever you two look at each other, but then they always have. I guess it's what's known as passion.'

'It's what's known as a clash of personalities.'

Jennifer laughed again. 'I can hear wedding bells. That church we've just come from would be perfect.'

Their father came over to join them. 'What are you two laughing about?' he asked, putting an arm around each of them.

'Jennifer is matchmaking again and she's not very good at it,' Charlotte murmured.

'How are things between you and Jordan?' her father asked immediately.

'The business is doing fine. He's very competent, as you know—'

'For once I wasn't talking about the business.' Simon winked. 'He's a good man, Charlie,' he said huskily. 'I always hoped you would settle down with someone like him.'

Charlotte was taken aback by that remark, but Jennifer grinned. 'There you go. I told you so,' she said, happily moving away to talk to one of her other guests.

'You like Jordan, then?' Charlotte asked her father carefully.

'Of course I like him; I've always liked him,' Simon said with a shake of his head.

'But...but what about the way he treated you?'

'What way?'

'Well...he made you sell the business out to him almost completely and you didn't want to.' Charlotte was very confused by her father's total lack of resentment at this. Back in France she had thought he was just putting on a brave face, acting like a gentleman, but now she wasn't so sure. 'I know you needed to retire, Dad, but he was a bit brutal,' she reminded him.

'Brutal? Jordan?' Simon shook his head. 'You've lost me, Charlie. Jordan didn't force me to do anything. I decided I needed to sell up. To be honest, I felt really ill and I didn't want to be at loggerheads with Ruth for a moment longer, so I jumped at his offer when he said he'd buy me out. It was a very generous offer as well, I can tell you.'

'I see.' Charlotte felt shell-shocked by the words. She glanced over at Jordan, who was chatting easily with Ruth now. And she remembered all the accusations she had thrown at him, all the times she had said he was cold and ruthless, and she felt a huge wave of remorse.

'I will give you my remaining shares in the company one day, Charlotte,' her father added softly. 'And I'm sorry I didn't hold on to more for you, but times were just a bit tight.'

'Heavens, Dad, that's the last thing on my mind.' Charlotte looked back at him swiftly. 'I'm just glad that you are happy and you are enjoying your retirement.'

He patted her back and moved away.

She looked over at Jordan again, knowing that she would have to apologise to him, and sooner rather than later. She recalled now how he'd told her he had treated her father fairly. But in her anger she hadn't listened. And because he had forced her into staying on with the company she had assumed he'd used similar tactics on her father—wrongly, as it turned out.

People were starting to leave. She noticed Jordan glancing at his watch. She'd have to go over now and apologise. She took a deep breath and walked over.

'Jordan, I—'

'I'm going to head back to London now, Charlie.'

'Are you?' She felt inordinately tongue-tied.

'Yes.' His eyes met hers directly. 'Do you want to come back with me so we can talk?'

'I…'

He raked a hand through the darkness of his hair. 'Look, if you want to leave the company then you can.'

The sudden words took her completely by surprise.

'You're right, I probably can find some other talented designer to take over the running of the department. If you want that job with David then take it.'

'Oh!' She felt her eyes glistening with tears. 'Well, thank you… I—'

'That's settled, then.' He nodded. 'Look, under the circumstances maybe you'd better not come back to London with me. We'll sort out details in the office tomorrow.'

As he turned to walk away Charlotte felt her heart thundering against her chest.

'Jordan, I'm sorry.' She called the words after him softly but he didn't seem to have heard her, because he kept on walking.

'Jordan.' After a few moments' trying to gather herself together she hurried after him. But he must have been walking very fast because there was no sign of him in the hallway. She was practically running now through the corridors and down to the foyer. There was a group of businessmen by the front door and she got slowed down trying to avoid bumping into them. And she was really afraid that when she got outside Jordan would be gone.

But as she stepped outside into the sunshine she saw him striding towards his car.

'Jordan, wait for me,' she called and raced down the steps.

He stopped and turned around with a look of surprise. 'What's wrong?'

'Everything.' She stopped beside him and looked up into his eyes. 'Jordan, I'm so sorry about everything, about accusing you of blackmailing Dad...' Her lips twisted in bitter disdain. 'That was a dreadful thing to say and I was so...so wrong.'

'He's told you, then?' Jordan asked steadily.

She nodded. 'I really am sorry. I was just so convinced because...'

'Because I blackmailed you into staying with the company.' He finished the sentence for her wryly. 'I know. And I'm sorry for that. You were right in some of the things you said to me. It wasn't a very honourable way of behaving...but I just didn't want to lose you.'

Charlotte felt her throat closing up with a fog of tears. If only he meant that in the way she wanted him to.

She took a step closer to him. 'And I'm sorry for the things I said earlier...about you being a viper and all... I am grateful for the way you acted towards Dad.'

'Don't go overboard, Charlie.' Jordan's tone hardened slightly. 'I don't want your gratitude. I never have.'

She bit down on her lip.

'Look, I'd better go.' He turned away from her to unlock his car.

'Back to London and Benita?' The question slipped out softly.

'London, yes, but not Benita.' He turned and looked at her then. 'What made you ask that?'

'I heard you had dinner with her last night at La Fortuna.'

'Who told you that?' Jordan frowned.

'Does it matter?'

'Well, yes, it matters, because it's not true. I didn't have dinner with Benita. I did, however, agree to meet her and her fiancé at the restaurant to give them the benefit of my opinion as an architect. They are thinking of buying it and wanted to know how big a job it would be to extend the premises.'

'Benita is getting married?'

Jordan nodded. 'Yes, to her childhood sweetheart. It's all over the papers today, but I guess you haven't read them.'

'No.' She swallowed hard. 'Are you upset?'

'Upset? What, that she's getting married?' Jordan smiled and shook his head. 'No, of course not. Why should I be?'

Why should he indeed? Jordan didn't lose his heart, he just moved on to the next conquest.

She shrugged. 'I just thought you might care for her, that's all.'

'You weren't jealous, were you?' He took a step closer to her.

'No!' Pride reared fiercely to her defence. 'No, of course not.'

'So that wasn't the reason you suddenly told me you wanted to leave the company on Friday night?'

She shook her head.

'Sure?' He reached out a hand and tipped her chin up so that she was forced to look at him. 'It's just that I did think we had been getting along together very well recently…and work has been running very smoothly.'

'Yes…we had and it was… I just…'

'Just miss David?' he finished for her.

'Not exactly.' Her eyes filled with sudden tears and she blinked them away furiously, cursing her hormones. Everything seemed to make her cry these days, and she wasn't used to feeling like this.

Steve's parents came out of the hotel and called goodbye to them. Jordan waved over cheerily and then opened the passenger door of his car for Charlotte. 'Come on, get in,' he said. 'I'll take you home.'

'Thanks.' She smiled shakily and got in. 'Just drop me at Jen's house; my things are still there.'

Jordan drove quickly down the narrow lanes and suddenly she realised with a start that they were on the wrong road. 'This isn't the way to Jen's house,' she said.

'I know that.'

'So where are we going?'

'Back to my place.'

She looked over at him with a frown.

'We need to talk properly, Charlie, and if we go back to your sister's place we'll be surrounded by people. We need some time alone.'

She fell silent, and suddenly felt nervous. If Jordan was just going to try and persuade her to stay on at the business he was wasting his time. She couldn't stay, not under the circumstances.

As the miles flicked by she tried to compose herself. Whatever happened she couldn't lose her cool, couldn't blurt out the truth. If he knew she was pregnant it would change everything. Maybe he would feel morally obliged to support her, but she didn't want someone in her life who just felt obligated towards her…who didn't love her.

So she would stay calm and remain firm about leaving the company.

'I have a buyer for my house in France,' Jordan told her suddenly.

She looked across at him in surprise. 'I didn't know you wanted to sell it.'

He nodded. 'I put it on the market when we were over

there. That was what I was doing in St Tropez before we left.'

'Oh, I see.' Suddenly she was remembering his daughter's bedroom, the teddy bears on the counterpane, the pictures on the dressing table...the look of pain in Jordan's eyes when he allowed himself to talk of her. And it added another painful dimension to the fact that she was pregnant with his child.

'So why have you decided to sell?' She hastily gathered herself together, trying to push the memory of that pretty little girl from her mind.

'I just decided it was time I moved on, forgot the past. It's held me back for long enough.'

'In what way?'

He shrugged. 'Since Natasha died and Nadine and I divorced, I haven't wanted anything serious in my life. I've had one meaningless fling after another. I've put business first at every juncture, and relationships firmly second. It's no way to live.'

'What's brought you to this conclusion?' Charlotte tried to keep her voice light.

'I thought that I wanted control of the business more than anything.' His voice softened as he glanced across at her. 'But the achievement feels empty at the moment. And I realise that success and business mean very little to me after all.

'You see, I've fallen in love, Charlotte,' he told her huskily.

It started to rain as Jordan pulled the car up outside his apartment. Large spots hit the windscreen in a sudden summer squall that seemed to echo the mood inside Charlotte perfectly.

'Who with?' She looked at him in dazed astonishment, her mind running through all the women he had so much as smiled at in the last few weeks. 'I thought you said you didn't mind about Benita getting married?'

'I don't.' He turned the engine of the car off and turned to look at her steadily. 'I'm not in love with Benita.'

The drumming of the rain on the roof of the car seemed to reach a wild crescendo that filled Charlotte's senses.

'So are you going to tell me who the lucky woman is?' she asked, her voice almost a whisper.

'I thought it was obvious.' His eyes drifted over her and then lingered softly on her lips. 'I'm in love with you, Charlotte. I think I have been from the first moment I set eyes on you. I was just too stupid, too blind to realise it.'

The husky words took a moment to register with her. She wondered if she had heard him properly. Maybe this was a dream and she was going to wake up at any moment?

'Look, I realise you are in love with David. I suppose I've known that from day one. And I shouldn't have tried to keep you the way I did...that business about making you stay on in the company for twelve months...' He shrugged awkwardly. 'It was a desperate attempt on my part not to lose you to him; I thought that if we were together every day you would get over him...'

'But I am over him,' she said softly. 'I was over David the day you took me out for dinner that first time...the night you took me to bed.'

'But I thought...' He frowned. 'I thought David was the reason you were leaving the business. Especially as you saw him on Friday night—the night you told me you wanted to leave.'

Charlotte shook her head. 'I never loved David. Not really, not madly and passionately and deeply. Not the way I love you.'

The words hung between them for a few moments and

then suddenly she was in his arms and he was holding her so close, so tightly that she could hardly breathe.

Then his lips found hers and he was kissing her with such passion that she felt alive with wonder and happiness.

'I keep thinking this is a dream,' she said shakily as he released her slightly. 'I thought you didn't believe in love any more. I thought that the only person you had ever loved was your ex-wife. And if it hadn't been for the death of your child…well, I suppose you'd be with her now…'

'Natasha's death did put an unbearable strain on our marriage. And soon after, I discovered that Nadine was seeing another man. I thought the affair was a result of her grief; she blamed herself such a lot. Natasha wasn't wearing her seat belt, you see.' He broke off abruptly. 'Anyway, I wanted to try and work through our grief, but it turned out she'd been seeing this guy even before the accident, so I suppose a divorce was looming regardless of what happened to Natasha.'

'I'm so sorry, Jordan.' Charlotte's eyes filled with tears.

'Hey, don't cry; it's in the past and we have the future to look forward to now.' He brushed the tears from her eyes and looked down at her with such tenderness that it made her want to cry all the more. 'Tell me again that you love me,' he demanded huskily.

'I love you so much it hurts,' she said breathlessly.

'And you don't have any feelings left for David at all?'

She shook her head. 'Not one.'

'God, and to think I've been trying to keep my distance from you for weeks to give you a chance to get over him! It's been sheer hell taking you out and bringing you home and not touching you… I've wanted you so much that it's been driving me almost insane with frustration and desire. I tell you, I never realised I had such strong will-power before.'

Charlotte laughed through a haze of tears. 'It's been the same for me. I've wanted you like crazy as well.'

Jordan bent and kissed her and for a long time they didn't speak. There was just the warmth of their kisses, and the bliss of being in each other's arms.

'We've wasted a lot of time, haven't we?' Jordan reflected as he pulled away from her. 'I wanted to ask you out from the moment I joined the company. But you were dating David and I told myself it was best that way—I sensed even back then that you had the word "serious" stamped all over you.'

Charlotte smiled tremulously.

'When I heard your relationship with David had finished I could hardly keep away from you. That day when I walked into your office and you were telling someone that there was a new man in your life, I was shattered and I knew without any doubt that I wanted you and had to try to get you.'

'I thought you'd only asked me out to find out if I knew anything about Dad's whereabouts,' she whispered unsteadily.

Jordan shook his head. 'I couldn't believe the bad luck of the timing of all that. You were so angry with me and all I wanted to do was take you into my arms.'

'I didn't mean to be angry with you. I guess I was fighting my growing feelings for you and I was just so desperately worried about Dad.'

He looked into her eyes. 'I know you were…and your fierce loyalty for people you care about is one of the reasons I love you so much.' He said the words with deep feeling.

'So you've forgiven me for all those awful things I said?'

'Absolutely. You will have to pay a few forfeits, of course…extra kisses, that kind of thing.' He grinned at her playfully. 'Shall we go inside and start making up for all that time we've wasted?' he added huskily.

Desire escalated inside her, she wanted him so much. But she needed to tell him that she was pregnant before they went any further.

She hesitated, trying to find the right words, suddenly feeling very shy.

'Come on, let's get inside while this rain has abated a little.'

Before she could stop him Jordan reached for the door handle and stepped out of the car.

There was nothing for it but to follow him. She'd tell him immediately they were inside, she told herself as they ran hand in hand through the rain. But once they were in the privacy of the lift Jordan started to kiss her with such a forceful, hungry passion that she was powerless to do anything but kiss him back.

When the doors opened he led her across the corridor and in through the door of his apartment with an impatience that made them both laugh breathlessly.

'Now, where was I?' he asked as soon as the door closed behind him. 'Somewhere about here, wasn't it?' He reached and found the sensitive area of her neck that he had been kissing in the lift. 'Or was it here?' he murmured, kissing her cheeks, her eyelids, her lips.

Instinctively she put her arms up around his shoulders, leaning closer, matching the kisses and loving the thrill of his body pressed close against hers. Then he picked her up and carried her through to his bedroom.

'Jordan, there is something I need to say,' she said nervously as he put her down on the bed.

'There's something I need to say as well,' he murmured, his hands moving with possessive ease over her body. She welcomed them, wanted to feel them more intimately. Her jacket was thrown to the floor and she felt his fingers brushing against her bare flesh as he drew the zip at the back of her dress down.

She quivered helplessly as his mouth left her lips to trail a string of kisses down her throat.

'This is really important,' she whispered, although a part of her wanted to just forget words and continue like this with seduction and warmth and sensations of love. But she had to tell him the truth and she had to tell him now.

'Jordan.' She pulled back from him. 'Jordan, I'm going to have your baby.' She blurted the words out before she lost her courage and she felt him go still beside her.

'I'm pregnant,' she whispered, looking into his eyes with apprehension.

To say he looked shocked was an understatement.

'It was a shock for me as well,' she murmured unsteadily. 'It was the reason I asked you to release me from our agreement. I was so scared and I didn't want you to feel trapped or obligated in any way. I still don't… Jordan, say something,' she whispered in anguish. 'I should have told you this downstairs in the car, shouldn't I?'

'You should have told me straight away,' he said gruffly.

'I only found out yesterday myself. But I'm really pleased about it…' Her eyes filled with tears. 'I really want to have your baby.'

'Oh, God, Charlotte.' He gripped her to him, holding her so tightly she could barely breathe.

'Does this change the way you feel about me?' she whispered tremulously.

'No! Why should it?' He pulled back from her then and she saw that his eyes were fervent with emotion. 'I love you, Charlotte, and having a baby together will be the most wonderful joy in the world to me.'

Suddenly they were kissing passionately, holding each other as if they would never let go. Charlotte was so relieved and her heart was so full of happiness she felt it was going to explode.

'I love you so much,' she whispered unsteadily. 'More than words can say. Will you make love to me?'

He stroked her face with one teasing, delicate finger. 'Only on one condition.'

She pulled away from him and looked at him with puzzlement.

'Say you'll marry me,' he said softly. 'Say you'll marry me as soon as we can possibly arrange it.'

She swallowed hard on a tight knot of emotion in her throat. 'Are you asking me this because I'm pregnant?' she whispered. 'Because—'

'I'm asking you because I love you, Charlotte.' He cut across her firmly. 'I love you and I want to spend the rest of my life with you.'

She brushed away the tears from her face. 'In that case the answer is yes, Jordan, let's get married.'

Jordan pulled her down with him so that they were lying on the bed. 'Now, where were we?' he murmured playfully, reaching to kiss her again.

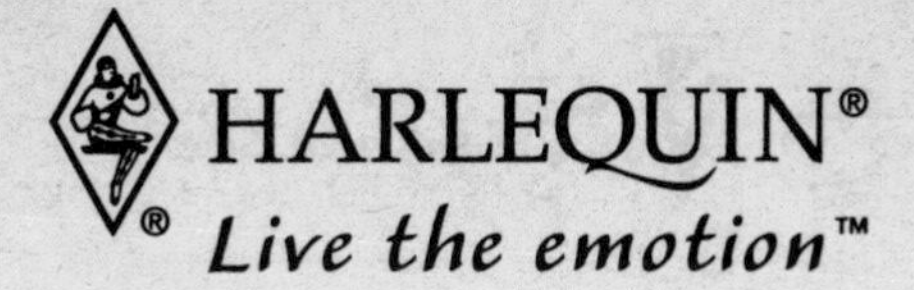

HARLEQUIN®
AMERICAN Romance®

Upbeat,
All-American Romances

HARLEQUIN®
flipside

Romantic Comedy

Harlequin Historicals®

Historical,
Romantic Adventure

HARLEQUIN®
INTRIGUE®

Romantic Suspense

HARLEQUIN®
HARLEQUIN ROMANCE®

The essence of
modern romance

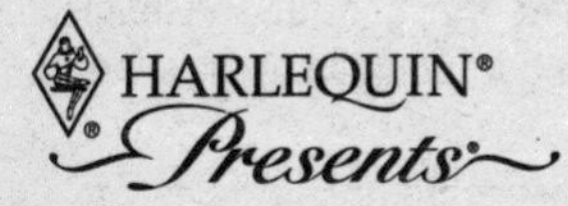

Seduction and passion
guaranteed

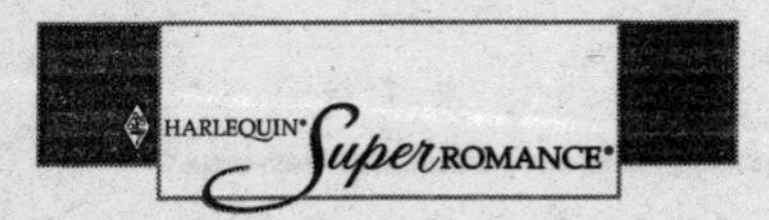

Emotional,
Exciting, Unexpected

Temptation®

Sassy, Sexy, Seductive!

www.eHarlequin.com

HDIR204